SCARLET hearts

BRITTON BRINKLEY

Scarlet Hearts

BRITTON BRINKLEY

LANDINGHAM STANLEY PRESS

O-H...

Author's Note

Scarlet Hearts wasn't a book that was supposed to exist. Then my bestie, my twin and fellow author Ashley Willow came to me and said "Hey, I want to you to apply to this signing with me but you have to have strong ties to Ohio, so I need you to write a book that takes place there." Too bad it wasn't enough that my alma mater is The Ohio State University. Yet, that was my inspiration for this spicy contemporary romance. Two people on the same campus, at the same places at the same time, but fate never brought them together through undergrad. The years pass and life happens and then randomly they find one another. Two hearts that bleed scarlet and gray finding their way to each other seemed like the perfect plot.

Now as I said, I did attend OSU some years ago. Some of the places, such as dorms were real to me then. Not everything in here is completely accurate to OSU's campus or even Columbus, but close enough that it works. Keep that in mind.

I hope you enjoy this little trip down nostalgia lane as much as I did.

<u>Trigger/Content Warnings:</u>

- Grief

- Death of a parent

- Tragic Death

- Infertility (mentioned)

- Miscarriages (mentioned)

- Graphic medical descriptions/conditions

- Healing from trauma/grief

- Explicit language

- Explicit sexual content

<u>For the most up-to-date list of content and trigger warnings:</u>

Chapter 1

LEIGHTON

LOSING A PARENT WRECKS you like getting struck by lightning, rolled over by a boulder, and drowned all at once. You can't breathe, you can't think. The only thing that exists is the never-ending pain holding you in place. The impossibly heavy anchor ensuring you suffocate beneath the surface rather than inhale normally again.

To do it once is hell.

To live it twice is crippling.

The woman left behind is a barely functioning drone shuffling through her days, clinging to a routine that barely keeps her afloat, but helps her forget it's just her now.

She is me.

I am her.

It's just me.

"Lee, it's been six months." The heartbreak in my best friend Allie Richards's voice nearly breaks me all over again. The press of my eyes closed only allowing her words to burrow deeper into what's left of me. No tsunami or hurricane could wash away her words, or my loss or the horrific memories.

"I know."

Allie's soul-crushing sigh only twists the knife in my gut. This conversation is the same one we have every day. The days pass, rolling into the next season, but the tone and message remain the same. "Honey, move here. I hate that you're up there all alone."

A humorless sniffle leaves me. "And do what?"

She only chuffs. Our regular album interlude ready for it's daily repeat. "You're a physician's assistant—against my wishes—you can do whatever you want."

"Allie..." The tears build behind my eyes again. Crying is all I seem to do these days. Followed by my endless wallowing, staring out the front windows as if my parents were going to come waltzing up my driveway any minute. The premier feature of living so close to the people I loved most.

As adults, we either drift away from our families or hold them so close that it's agony when it's time to let go. I'm a case of the latter. My parents have always been my universe outside of school and work. A life without them seems cruel.

It's an endless purgatory of emptiness coupled with an overwhelming sense of drowning all at once, every second of every day.

Whatever I did in a past life to deserve this, I'm so sorry.

There's nothing in this world I wouldn't trade to get them back.

There wasn't a day that went by without an unannounced visit from my mom and dad. They didn't care if I was actually home or not. As if my home was theirs, they would just let themselves in and get comfy. If I was on shift, I came home to a clean house and a home-cooked meal. Otherwise, we watched belly-ache-inducing game shows and played every board game known to man. It was a simple life, but a good one.

I miss them. They were the greatest people. Just two people in love with life and each other, eager for a large family. But fate had other plans; I was the only miracle child. In that way, we're the same; they were only children too. With the two of them gone, there's just me up here in the middle of nowhere.

My grandparents died when I was young, and any other cousins or great-relatives are so distant they may as well not exist.

"Don't Allie me. Mike and I are coming out this weekend. I'm really worried about you." I can't stand when she gives me that pitying tone mixed with momma-knows-best. It makes it hard to go against her requests. Not that she was any different back when we were college freshmen living in the same suite.

Allie has always been the dominant my-way-or-the-highway type in our nearly two-decade-long friendship.

"Are you bringing the kids?" I perk up just a fraction, hoping the answer is yes. My nieces are the cutest and the only cure besides blood and guts for the painful existence I now trudge through with each new dawn.

"Hell no! We need time without them, and *you* need us. But..." The pitch of her voice rises. Without even seeing her face, I know the grin she's wearing. That hear-me-out lilt that always accompanied her endless list of reasons to move back to Ohio. "If you come here, then you can see them anytime."

The words wash over me in a whimsical tune. It's the same one she's been using since we graduated fifteen years ago and I moved back to New York. No doubt there's another house somewhere along her street for sale she's going to try to talk me into buying.

It never mattered what house she and Mike moved into around Columbus, Ohio, and its suburbs, Allie Richards found one within walking distance of theirs. Each one somehow outfitted with my non-negotiables for a home.

I guess that's what best friends do. *No*, that's what mine does.

Giving in quickly so as not to draw out this whole interaction, I forcefully release a defeated breath. "Okay, which one is it?"

I swear I know every house in their neighborhood. It's the longest they've lived in one place, enough time passing that I fell in love with the community and even formed friendships with some of the women on her street. Allie has never said it, but I think having my nieces finally made them settle.

"Do you remember the neighbors on the right who remodeled the exterior to look like a modern farmhouse?"

A bolt of lightning shoots through me, a stiff rod lengthening my spine as I balance on the edge of the sofa. There's no way I could forget. Their update was as if they dove into my dreams and extracted the home I always imagined for myself.

I stared at that exterior so many nights it's committed to memory. There was a perfect view from the grassy knoll that trisects the street beside Allie and Mike's corner lot. A view so perfect at times I convinced myself my friends bought their house just for me to someday enjoy it.

Visions of that beauty dance through my mind now. The blue siding, natural-stained wood shutters, and matching double front doors are a sight to behold. Pristine white railings bordering the wrap-around porch tie the whole look together. Then there are the custom rocking chairs on the front porch, serving as the perfect cherry on top.

Its newfound beauty sets the house apart. An anomaly nestled into a block of historical homes all but boasting of its uniqueness.

The couple who lives there has thirty years on us, but they've always been friendly. Thanks to their property essentially sharing the corner lot spot with Allie's, we've been invited for countless bonfires and cocktail nights in their sprawling backyard. A perfect rectangle bordered with flower beds the wife, June, planted when they first settled in.

"Of course."

She squeals, "It's on the market!"

My teeth sink into my bottom lip, my spine stretching a fraction straighter.

I always told Allie if they sold that house, I'd buy it in a heartbeat. It's always been the truth, but now that my fantasy is staring back at me, it seems odd to jump. Almost as if it's wrong to be so excited about leaving my roots behind.

"Lee..." My nickname drawn out in that come-on-you-know-you-want-to-do-it tone, only drives my teeth deeper into my plump bottom lip. The pressure just forceful enough I'm one more surprise away from breaking through the skin.

"Send me the link."

It won't hurt to look. Though I know every exterior detail and the entire first floor, my heart hammers in my chest.

The sight of that masterpiece will hit differently now.

Now someone like me could have it as their own. *I could* have it. Live there. Make new memories within its walls. The do-over Allie says I so desperately need.

She's not wrong. In my gut, I know that a fresh start is, truthfully, a change I've needed for some time. It's my heart that gives me pause. That dreaded lump of muscle shouting against the pain with every thought of moving on without them.

Another squeal bursts through my earbud, so loud I have to pull it out. "We're going to be neighbors!"

"Maybe," I warn, keeping my tone noncommittal. "I gotta go."

"Don't walk too far!"

A soft chuckle leaves me as I involuntarily shake my head. "Love you, Crazy."

"Love you too, Bedbug. It's going to be okay."

Then the line goes dead.

Another humorless laugh bursts free, thinking of the nicknames we've been calling each other since we were eighteen years old. Names that mean nothing to anyone but us anymore.

One of our floormates hadn't been happy when we told him off for trying to sleep with every chick on the floor. The bastard had shouted down the hall how we were both crazier than bedbugs, and thus, Allie became Crazy, and I became Bedbug. No point in letting some guy's derogatory name-calling go to waste.

Slouching against the couch cushions, my gaze catches on my sneakers. The damn shoes glaring at me as if they know I'm debating not going for my daily hot girl walk—the term used by the twenty-something women who prance around my hospital. The only thing that's kept me sane for the past six months.

My mother's tragic death devastated me. Like Allie, she was a daredevil. She skydived and skied, and cliff jumped and rode four-wheelers like no one's business, but it was a hit and run while she was walking through the grocery store parking lot that took her from us.

With her departure only minutes before closing time and the store practically empty, hours passed before a worker found her. Body contorted and face a bloody mess, she'd lain there on the cold pavement unable to call for help. By the time she reached the hospital, there wasn't much the doctors could do.

Internal bleeding is the silent killer.

Dad was one of those matter-of-time deaths. He was never particularly great at taking care of himself, which only got worse after Mom died. But he, too, lived life to the fullest. He didn't care that his heart and kidneys were failing or that he'd been a diabetic his whole life. Dad made the seconds count.

The last time they admitted him to the hospital, only fourteen months after Mom died, I knew he wasn't coming home. He'd gotten too sick, and the staff was having to pull every stop to keep his body functioning as well as it could. Though Dad's death hit me hard, too, his was easier to work through. I at least got to watch him fight for another four weeks before I lost him.

There was time to prepare. Time to say goodbye. Time to accept that once he was gone, it would be just me, and there was nothing I could do about it.

So here I am alone in upstate New York while my best friend since college tries to convince me to move back to Ohio for the billionth time. Home of my alma mater, The Ohio State University. The only place I ever felt like myself.

Truthfully, the only place that ever felt like home.

My phone vibrates with a text. A link to the house with a winky emoji from Allie filling the screen.

Clicking the link, a choked cough barks free. The sale price is much lower than I would have expected. Biting my lip again, I scroll through the pictures, my jaw dropping instantly.

I've been in their home countless times, but it seems they've also redone the inside since I was last there. How long ago was that?

Two years, maybe.

It's literally everything I've ever dreamed of. It's the do-over I need.

When the stars seem to align, and all we have to say is *yes*, we either hesitate or we jump.

Me: I'll call the realtor in the morning.

Allie: That was easy

Me: What do I have to lose?

Chapter 2

LEIGHTON

2 MONTHS LATER...

I never knew I had so much shit.

Books. Boots. Jeans. Sneakers—okay, those I knew about. But where did all this other stuff come from?

Just random things I've collected since college with each new apartment or house I rented. Quadruples of the same pan. Eight sets of dishes—each with enough settings to serve at least twelve people.

I've never even had more than three guests over for dinner at a time.

Spinning to observe the rest of my things littering the room only draws my brow higher. More boxes cover almost every square foot of the first floor. How does someone not realize that they inadvertently became a hoarder?

It's clear I have from the two massive boxes of sheets and three more with blankets. There are enough T-shirts to supply a school and plenty of candles to burn down the entire state—each one brand new. I have a habit of picking up at least five on every trip to the store, but I never light them.

"Auntie Lee, you have so many books," my niece Victoria whines. The *so* stretched out longer than it took her to sing *Barbie Girl* earlier. My little goofy drama queen. A soul destined to be an actress in horror movies or heartbreaking romances.

Though she has voiced her complaints about every five minutes, she hasn't slowed her pace. Each book pulled from the boxes one by one before stacking them in neat color-coded piles. Of course, she picked the one with my dark romance novels this time. Many with covers she has no business viewing. But such is life.

Tori insisted on helping because I was her favorite aunt—her uncle's wives don't count, according to her. In truth, it was the easiest way to keep the seven-year-old occupied.

"I know, baby. Better to get lost in a book than the real world."

Her blonde brows scrunch low, the purse of her petite mouth causing me to cover mine, stifling what's sure to become a belly-aching laugh. But she continues with her task. Her narrow shoulders shimmy as she hums the beat to yet another pop song, unbothered by my wisdom, oblivious to my barely contained cackle.

One day, those words will make sense to her, but for today, I'm just her crazy aunt who says weird things. A reminder she gives me constantly.

"Ma'am, the bedroom furniture is done," the movers announce, entering the living room.

Their postures sag, navy blue shirts stuck to their opposing frames—one lithe and one thicker in build. Their eyes droop with exhaustion while they nearly sway on their booted feet. Each thick droplet of sweat lining their brows and streaking down their temples noted.

The temperature was in the fifties last week, and then suddenly, two days ago, it dropped to the twenties—a recipe for me to crank up the heat.

This winter's weather has been insane, a constant seesaw of two extremes. It will undoubtedly fill the ED with sick patients. Stuffy noses and discarded wet tissues at every turn. Uncovered coughs and a slew of antibiotics dispensed.

Thanks a lot, Mother Nature!

Fortunately, unpacking and relaxation are all I need to worry about for the next few weeks. A break I'm sure I need whether I'm ready to embrace it or not. Rhinovirus will just have to wait.

"Thank you. Have a great rest of the day." The young guys smile and wave with their departure just as Mike stumbles through the front door with their elder daughter, Abigail, in tow. Large brown bags are cradled under both his arms, with a slightly smaller one clutched to Abby's chest.

The scent of grease, egg rolls, and fried rice overwhelms my senses. My tongue all but lolling out of my mouth as I salivate. Thankfully, the rumble of my stomach is hidden by Tori once again singing *Barbie Girl* and Allie yelling from around the corner. It's pure, utter chaos. But I feel more grounded than I have in a really long time.

"Oh! Food!" Tori cheers, abandoning the newly opened box she'd been working on and charging toward the kitchen.

It was the first room Allie insisted we put together despite my inability to cook more than ramen, spaghetti, or soup in the crock pot.

My girl is a genius. It kept us out of the way as the furniture was brought in. Each new medium box emptied, hitting me with a burst of adrenaline and accomplishment.

Allie is meticulously organized in her kitchen. We opened one box at a time, her scrutinous eye inspecting each utensil, plate, pan, and mug. If the item didn't pass her test, it ended up in the donation boxes Mike will drop off for me tomorrow.

For the first time since I've been on my own after college, I got rid of things I didn't need instead of collecting more. A feeling of shedding weight rushed through me. A lightness I hadn't felt in some time. The perfect beginning to this fresh start.

"Hands!" Allie shouts behind her daughter. The hearty rush of water hitting our ears only moments later. Only now, she has switched songs, singing the lyrics to what I'm pretty sure is a Disney hit.

"Hey, honey." Mike slides up next to Allie as she shuffles from around the corner. He presses a soft kiss to her cheek and then her mouth. A look shared between them that makes me feel like an intruder. As if I'm a child witnessing something I shouldn't.

The two are the cutest fucking pair I've ever seen. Allie is definitely the dominant personality in the relationship, but Mike treats her like an absolute queen.

Mike's eyes twinkle with mirth as he continues to stare down at his wife. Unspoken words shared between them before he pecks her lips again, the two of them giggling in unison. He readjusts the massive bag under his arm when Allie drapes an arm around his middle, pulling him into her side.

It's nauseating but still brings out that little green monster of jealousy. Not of them exactly, but people who have someone in their corner, no matter what. I had my parents and now I don't.

There's Allie, too, but it's not quite the same. My friend isn't mine to keep.

It's not that I didn't have opportunities for relationships; I had plenty. They just never worked out. They were too invested in their careers, or I was. I moved too slowly, or they weren't interested enough. I was never going to be a traditional wife, staying home and cooking and cleaning, but that's what they wanted. The list goes on. After a while, it just became easier to stay single. Then my parents both died, and having a man in my life was the last thing I was thinking about.

"Give me the food. That way, you two can make out as long as you want." I snatch the bags from Mike, swiftly turning on my heel toward the kitchen.

"You know now that you live here, I can set you—"

Poking my head back around the doorway, I glare at my best friend. This is another of her many quirks. She has tried to set me up with countless men over the years. Anything to get me married, too. Bonus if they were also in Ohio.

"Allison Elaine Richards, if you finish that sentence, I swear..." The twist of my neck to the side with my eyes pressed shut so harshly the muscles vibrate like strings on a guitar.

The slow peel of my eyelids opening reveals her grin as she wraps her arms around Mike's narrow waist. "You'll what?"

I've got nothing. She knows that. I never have a good retort or reason to go against every ridiculous idea she has. So I only sigh while shuffling into the kitchen.

Unpacking the endless containers will take my mind off my loneliness.

Abby and Tori have already opened a container of chicken fried rice and started digging in, their forks full, as they eye me warily. Both with cheeks puffed out like chipmunks, bodies frozen as if paralyzed.

"Keep eating!" I encourage them. Their mother is going to have a heart attack, but it pays to be the fun aunt.

There aren't a lot of moments when my carefree side comes out these days, but with those two little gremlins, it always does. Their bright smiles can always pull out my laughter or the goofy faces that involve me contorting my features so harshly the muscles ache.

By the time Allie and Mike join us in the kitchen, I've already started eating, too. My fork digging into multiple containers to match my favorite girls. They giggle and crack jokes while Allie tries not to blow a gasket at how uncouth we're being. Mike only laughs, joining in the fun. He's been with Allie for nineteen years now. He knows how to just go with the flow. Life's easier for everyone if we do.

It doesn't take us long to eat and then clean the kitchen. Our agreement to get back to work unanimous. Each of us disappears to a different corner of the house to continue our quest of unpacking all the meaningless stuff I've collected.

"Okay, guys. Enough."

Allie's vibrant blue eyes meet mine. "We're not even halfway."

"Crazy, take the girls home. It's after nine." Her mouth opens, but I quickly cut off whatever argument she has. "No. You've done enough."

A flinch shoots Mike's shoulders high around his ears. His wide eyes darting between me and his wife as if unsure who will win this fight.

"Fine," Allie grimaces. "Mike, get the girls."

Tori has been passed out on the couch for over an hour. One leg hanging off the edge and the other over the arm. Her blonde hair twisted into a rat's nest beneath her. Abby also abandoned us, choosing to curl up in my bed and watch movies.

"Thank you guys for helping," I hug Allie close.

"Of course. I'll be back in the morning."

Throwing her a wry look, she only quirks a brow, planting a hand on her hip. "That's not up for debate."

"Yeah, okay," I agree, pulling her into me again, the tougher version of myself once again tucked away. The sting of tears builds behind my eyes. She's all I have left now. The sister I never had. The one who will also never leave my side. Blood couldn't have made us any closer.

Her hands rub up and down my back. "Oh, sweetie, you're going to be okay. You're here now, so I can take care of you."

With a sniffle, I pull away. "That's not your job."

Her shrug only makes me chuckle. "True, but if you won't take any of the men I throw your way, who else will?"

Then she's gone, skipping across our yards with a backward wave once she reaches her front door.

Damn, it sucks that she's right.

Chapter 3

GAVIN

My knees ache as I pound the pavement. Every strike reminds me I am not getting any younger. Neither is my body, apparently. A youth full of contact sports did a number on me. But without my morning runs, my days don't start off on the right foot. Literally.

Downtown Columbus seems to wake up just as early as any other major city these days. When they finally started rebuilding, it became a hot spot for those thriving in their twenties and thirties—a prime location for businesses, bars, and restaurants.

Traffic lines the streets. The sounds of rumbling engines, screeching brakes, and honked horns combine to drown out the music blasting in my ears. Miraculously, I can still hear everything, despite the high volume of my earbuds. Each warning from my phone about prolonged exposure being "bad" for me ignored.

I don't care.

I need this.

These precious miles are my reset.

My time to obsess over all the ways I've fucked up my life over the years.

A process that should keep me from spiraling into a pity party—it often does. I have a good life. Solid career, great friends, and a nice condo. I travel and have a loving family. But there are always things we wish we'd done differently. Chances we never took that leave us wondering "what if" and wrong turns we don't understand making.

I snort to myself, turning down a side street and picking up speed. It's always the same damn thoughts funneling through my head. Records on repeat blaring through my mind.

A stretch of shade looms ahead. The chill is sure to work its way deeper into my bones despite the sweat already plastering my clothes to my body. On frigid days like this, it's night and day between the sunshine and the cover of the trees—the beauty of living in the Midwest.

Another cold front rolled in. That crisp scent of snow filling the air.

It's no matter; I'll run in any weather. All I need are my tennis shoes and deafening music.

Heavy hip-hop beats thrum against my eardrums. There's no comprehension of what the words are, only that the bass pushes me forward.

Or maybe it's away.

Most days, it's unclear if I'm running away from my mistakes or aiming for a future I always envisioned for myself.

Tucking my chin, I push harder. Every muscle quivers against the increase in speed and power, but I ignore it. I can't be in my own head today, and this is the only way to clear it.

Twenty minutes later, I'm entering my building panting as if I've never done any activity. Checking my smartwatch, my mileage is a solid five above what it usually is. It would be easier to ignore the reason why, but that has never served me well, either.

It's the failure that burns me the most. That ever-present emptiness forever taunting me.

I gave twelve years of my life to that woman. Some were happy, others weren't.

Plenty of couples fall out of love. But it's five years later, and I'm still heartbroken. I am still a lost, wandering puppy trying to find purpose in losing the only woman I've ever loved. Trying to understand how the plan could be for me to live this lonely life without someone to call my own.

It hits me hardest at this time of year. The holidays are a constant reminder of what I can't seem to find.

Then there's Valentine's Day. That hallmark-infested day that I've always loved. Even when I was younger, I would always bring every friend and classmate Valentine's cards and candy. I would shower women I knew with flowers and chocolates, all because love might be my favorite thing in the world.

Call me a pansy. Call me a hopeless romantic. It doesn't matter. I am. I always have been.

Stepping into my apartment, I swipe the back of my hand across my upper lip, wiping away the thick line of sweat that collected there.

"What took you so long?"

I can only groan, hearing my sister's voice drift from the living room. She does this all the time. Just shows up and parks herself on my couch. I shouldn't expect anything else since she's attending OSU for grad school. I never thought my baby sister would want to follow in my footsteps, but she did for both college and now for her graduate studies.

"Ember, why are you here? I need to get ready for work."

My feet move in a mere shuffle as I enter the living area. She props herself up on her knees, elbows resting on the back edge of the couch, those big innocent doe eyes staring back at me. "Hello to you too." Her signature snort, making the corner of my mouth twitch with amusement.

"I don't recall you greeting me that way," I huff.

These are the type of siblings we are. Faked exasperation, knowing there's nothing but love between us. We've always had a more playful relationship despite our age difference. A reality I would never change.

"Stop being a grouch, Gav. I just came to make sure you're coming to my event this weekend."

My eyes press shut. Ever since Jen and I broke up, my sister has dragged me to this damn party on Valentine's Day. Yes, I love the holiday, but what I don't love is joining my sister at a singles meet and greet and being reminded that I'm still alone. Painfully and embarrassingly so.

The first year, I didn't put up a fight. My sister is proud of the organization she and her girlfriends started in undergrad, which catered to young professional singles getting together for adventures all over Ohio.

Did they invent the wheel? *No*, but it was a brilliant idea, nonetheless. I'm so proud of her. The experience will serve her well as she enters the non-profit sector after her graduate program.

However, this year, I was hoping she'd forget or not ask or something—anything so I wouldn't have to stand in that room, engulfed by the reminder that so many of my friends have someone, and I don't. Not to mention, it's not cool to go to singles events with your little sister, who's twelve years younger than you.

I had the plan worked out in my head: I would marry straight out of college, enjoy life with my wife for a few years, and then have a big family. It was something I always wished Ember and I had.

My beautiful wife and I would have a few dogs, a big house, and vacation in all of our favorite places. We'd dance in the kitchen late at night and sit on the porch watching the sunrise. We'd spend quiet Friday nights curled up on the couch and chilly fall nights at football games for our sons. Only for me to be the loudest Dad cheering at our daughter's dance recital.

Back then, I also figured I would move my family back to the country where I'm from. It would prove to be a quieter life, but one where our kids and animals had land to play on like I did when I was young. Unfortunately, there's not much of a market for corporate CPAs in the middle of nowhere.

A heavy sigh leaves me, my hands scrubbing my face. My skin is only slightly warmer now, despite the heat pelting me. "Em, I love you, but I would prefer not to."

That pout she's given me since she was born appears. The expression she knows always makes me cave. I would do anything for my baby sister, and she knows it. Exploits it.

"Gav, I just don't want you to be at home alone... sulking." Her nose scrunches as if witnessing a putrid smell. The urge to sniff my pits to check if it's me making my fingers twitch at my sides.

Once again, my eyelids press shut against her words, my shoulder blades dropping against the wall behind me. That was my exact plan. Watch some romance movies and grumble about not having love in my life. Maybe even order pizza instead of eating my normal meal of grilled chicken and veggies on a Friday night.

Fuck, I am so pathetic.

Those doe eyes meet mine again, and I know I won't tell her no. I can't. I never could. "On one condition," I relent. She perks up, a wide grin pulling at her cheeks. The vibrant rosy hue continuing to glow against her pale skin from braving the cold.

Our mother used to say I stole all her melanin—not that we had much. Though my mother is from Bahrain, she's almost as pale as my dad, a country boy from the middle of nowhere Ohio. I'm the only one of us four that has any real color.

But where I got the complexion from Mom's side, I got Dad's icy blue eyes. A shade Jen used to call artic. Add in the well-trimmed beard I've let grow in, and I look more exotic than I have a right to.

"Are you going to tell me?" she asks. I shake my head. Of course I had been lost in memories of my ex again.

"*You...*" I point a finger at her. "...keep your friends away from me."

An audible scoff ricochets through the room. "Oh, come on!" Ember's hands fly up in the air, eyes rolling. "Kimmie's been in love with you since I was a freshman. I can't do anything about that."

"Ember." My tone a warning. Of course, she would defend her friend who practically throws herself at me every time she sees me, all but spreading her legs and saying put a baby in me.

Wait. She did do that once.

Shaking my head again, I do my best to clear away that memory as a shudder works its way through my body.

"Okay. Okay." Ember pats the air in front of her, palms facing me in a placating gesture. "I'll tell her she can't have your dick."

An even more exasperated groan leaves me. It drives me insane that my sister is as crass as I am. I must have rubbed off on her too much as a kid, blasting my rap music and the explicit songs we used to listen to.

"Get out."

"Ugh, fine. Pick me up at five on Friday. I have to be there early to make sure everything is set up properly."

She hops from the couch, stopping in front of me before wrapping her arms around my middle. "I love you, Gav."

Holding her back, I let my cheek fall to the top of her head. "Love you too, but really, you need to go. I need to get ready for work."

She sniffs once. "You're right. You stink more than usual today."

Shoving at her shoulder lightly, she only cackles, leaving me groaning again. Her skipping steps carrying her out of my apartment with nothing but a wide grin on her face.

I am going to regret this. I just know it.

Chapter 4

LEIGHTON

"Lee!" Allie calls, barging in through my front door.

"In here."

She enters the living room, finding me sprawled out on the floor. I've been here since I got home from my shift an hour ago.

Being a medical professional is not for the faint of heart or the bleeding ones most days. It's challenging but rewarding work. Yet, no matter which way you spin the positives, it doesn't change how much it takes from you. Every interaction, procedure, conversation, diagnosis, and held retort strips you of your energy. They compile over the hours, wearing you down mentally, emotionally, and physically until you're barely a shell of yourself flopping onto your bed once you walk through your front door.

I've been in busy emergency departments before, but damn, today felt like a war zone. Maybe that's because I haven't worked in a month.

Lead weighed down my limbs as I stumbled out to my car this evening. Everything in me was stripped so clean that the living room was as far as I made it.

"Why are you on the floor? Please don't tell me I need to get down there with you."

Sitting up, I shove to my feet, ungracefully plopping onto the couch. Four ragged breaths rumble through me before I can settle against the cushions. "I'm so tired," I whine, letting my head fall to her shoulder.

"Oh baby," she coos, patting my cheek. "Do you go in tomorrow?"

I can only nod. The sting of tears building behind my sleepy eyes, imagining another repeat of the twelve hours I just barely survived.

The schedule, truthfully, isn't bad. I work Monday through Thursday; then I'm off again until Monday. A perfect setup so I can spend Valentine's Day with my nieces. A surprise I've been planning with the girls so Allie and Mike can have some alone time. It's also just an excuse to buy us cute pajamas and scarf down junk food.

"So then you'll be off this weekend?"

"Uh, yeah…" My pulse kicks up a few notches, hoping one of the girls didn't spoil the surprise. It wouldn't be the first time those tiny lips let a secret spill free.

"Okay, that's perfect. I have an idea, and I need you not to say no."

"Uh…"

"I will take that as an agreement." Allie smiles widely, turning to face me on the couch so her knee knocks into me. The soft *thunk* of bone against bone only reminding me of the heinous femur fracture we had first thing this morning. "So I was at the grocery store today and ran into an old acquaintance. She was telling me about this singles club that does shit all over Ohio. Sounds like a blast if you like people."

I lick my lips, already not liking where this is going. A threatening stare narrows on me. No doubt Allie knows I'm already formulating an excuse to shut down whatever proposition she is about to sling my way.

"Anyway, they are having an event Saturday night downtown. It's supposed to be one of their biggest of the year. And since you're new here, well, kind of, it would be perfect to meet some new people."

"Did you hit your head today?"

"Don't give me that lip. Seriously, Lee, you can't just sit in your house all alone and work nonstop. You've been doing that for years."

"I have you and my nieces. I'm not alone."

The words are automatic despite feeling the most alone I have in my entire life.

Allie faces forward again, pulling my head to rest against the knob of her shoulder. She's silent as she runs a hand over my newly straightened hair. A soothing touch you'd give your child when they're scared or sick.

My eyelids flutter shut, my nose burning, attempting to hold back the tears.

"I need you to hear me when I say this," Allie all but whispers. "I love you. My girls love you. Mike loves you. Your friends, whom you don't keep up with, love you. You can pretend like you're fine to everyone else, but I see right through you. I know you're sad. I know you feel lost and if you really don't want to go, I would never force you, but I think you've shut the world out for a long time. Maybe it's time to open the door on it again. If it works, great. If it doesn't, then you can still be my first-pick babysitter."

A wet laugh leaves me, my sleeve swiping under my eyes to dry my tears.

As pushy and ridiculous as Allie can be, no one has a heart as big as her. She's been there for every one of my highs and lows. I should have known my humor wouldn't be enough to throw her off my scent. They say no one knows you like your best friend, and it's true.

Her intentions are good, so maybe, for once, I can just go along with one of her plans without argument.

"I'll go, but I have nothing to wear."

"I figured. Mike has the kids. Let's go."

She laughs at my pronounced groan as she tugs me off the couch with a swift pat on my butt cheek.

I am going to regret this.

As a person who loves to shop, I loathe physically going to stores. The lines and swarms of people only add to my agitation and thunderous heart rate. And without a doubt, there's always a sea of children screeching and running through the place like they've never left home.

Who wouldn't dislike the crowds, rude customers, and smells?

I get more than enough unpleasant scents while working. There's no need to add them to retail therapy.

Over the past few years, online ordering has become my way of life, so ripping through the mall as Allie dragged me along was more than I bargained for.

Fortunately, my best friend has a keen eye. The type that can spot exactly what she's looking for before you have a moment to blink. We'd been in and out of the dress store so quickly my head spun.

A laundry list of preparatory things filled our ride home. Shave my legs, pluck my eyebrows, deep condition my hair, shave my pits and my vagina. *"Lee, I know it's a damn forest down there. Tidy it up in case you meet Mr. Right."*

It was exhausting and intrusive. From anyone else, I would have told them exactly where they could shove their advice, but not Allie. My best friend just makes me feel exposed, like I'm transparent to the entire world, and like so many things since my parents passed, I don't know how to handle it.

It took some convincing, but Allie dropped me off at home before pulling into her driveway. I'd barely tumbled through the front door with my bags when my phone vibrated in my pocket.

Allie: CLEAN IT UP!!! I mean it!

Practically tossing my phone across the room, I needed a few minutes to collect myself. Just some peace and quiet to process what I agreed to. For her. Not for me, I told myself.

In truth, my stomach was in knots, and my heart raced as I considered the many ways this could be a disaster.

Hours of staring at the wall did nothing to stifle the anxiety that raced through my veins, so now I'm here curled up on my couch watching chick flicks as if they're the key to me surviving a Valentine's Day party.

My teeth dig into my lip, nibbling at it while I take mental notes of the cute things these women say to the gorgeous, rich, charming men they always seem to attract.

A mirror to the fantasies I live on the pages of the novels filling my house.

There's a reason we all cling to happy endings. They make us believe we can heal from the hurt and live happy, fruitful lives. Especially once you've found the one who will turn your world upside down and move heaven and earth to make you smile.

It's bullshit.

For me, at least.

I've never been like these women in my books or movies. Hot men don't just fall into my lap. My brains and smile might lure them in, but the core of who I am sends them packing. A woman who possesses a heart that never lets anyone close could never keep the men we dream about. Not because I push them away but because I don't feel the way others do.

One of my college mentors noticed that quality in me. She was a cold, detached, but brilliant woman. *"You'll make a skilled physician, Leighton,"* she said.

"Why?" I questioned.

"Because you don't just know how to turn your emotions off; they never find you in the first place. It will keep you from getting attached. From making mistakes."

At the time, I was proud of the trait.

It's what I needed to be great at my profession of choice.

But now, as I sit alone on my couch, watching lovey movies and shoveling tortilla chips into my mouth, I hate that part of me.

There's no point in me watching these movies in hopes of doing all the right things and finding someone.

I'll probably never be able to love them, anyway. Life has proven this time and time again.

Loneliness and my nieces are all that wait for me.

Chapter 5

LEIGHTON

GOLD HAS ALWAYS BEEN my formal wear color. The vibrancy is a perfect complement to my toffee complexion. It is one of the few shades that gives me the appearance of glowing rather than washing out my yellow undertones.

But red...

Other than my Ohio State gear, I don't wear red. It always seemed to wash me out or make me feel too seen. The exact thoughts floating through my mind as I waddle walk in the monstrously high gold pumps Allie insisted on, doing my best to avoid the clumps of melted snow from the storm we had two days ago.

Only my best friend could have found a form-fitting red satin dress with gold embroidery that makes my curves pop in all the right ways. The thin straps that curve over my shoulders and split in two across my back hardly seem sufficient to hold up my decently sized boobs propped up high in the cups of the bodice. A bodice that reminds me of lingerie instead of cocktail attire.

If murder was legal, I might kill my friend.

Damn you, Allie, I nearly bark as a car flies by, almost spraying me with murky snow water. The small wave crashing to the sidewalk less than an inch away from where I slip and slide across a thick patch of ice.

My balance rights itself just in time to unravel once more. "Shit!" I grunt, my heel nearly slipping out from underneath me as I turn the corner toward the venue.

Lucky me, I had an Uber driver who couldn't figure out how to get on the right side of the street. My frustration grew until I finally jumped out the back to walk around the block.

Even several entrances down, the heavy beats of music pump through my chest. A match for my racing heart. Whether from my near-death fall or the anxiety of having to talk to new people, I'm unsure. Either way, I know I don't want to be here.

A gust of wind sweeps back the edges of my thick coat. The buttons undone only seconds after climbing into my Uber. Yes, it's brutally cold outside, but there was no need to set the temperature to extra high molten lava.

Smoothing my hands down the front of my dress, I take a deep breath before stepping inside.

A popular hip-hop song blares through the speakers. The artist and title escape me as my gaze widens, raking over the space. The pink and purple lighting turning its interior into more of a club than the bar it's listed as.

Groups of people nearly fill the room's open floor plan. Each cluster is a combination of animated laughter, wild gestures, and drinks in hand.

There's no rhyme or reason to the demographic. A noted point that has me biting my lip observing the ages, ranging from early twenties to maybe their sixties.

I'm lost in the sight before me, fascinated by the number of people willingly engaging in conversations and swaying to the beat of the music. My body flinching wildly when a man's voice sounds at my side. "Would you like to check your coat?"

I only awkwardly smile and nod as I shrug out of the wool peacoat, taking the numbered ticket he hands me. "Thanks." I raise the tiny sliver of paper that will be nearly impossible for anyone to keep up with plastering on a close-lipped smile.

His broad Hollywood award-winning grin hits me. "Have a great evening."

I only nod again before moving further into the space.

Booths line the outer edge, with small circular high-top tables through-out the middle. The clearing that's turned into what I assume is an unin-tentional dance floor bordering them at the front. With comfortable sitting areas nestled toward the back it gives the illusion of privacy. A dark corner meant to provide a secluded spot for those who might find connections tonight.

Flowers in white, red, and pink varieties adorn almost every surface, turning the room into an aromatic garden. Inhaling deeply, it reminds me of the many flower beds I often paused to admire around Ohio State's campus throughout my four years there. A shining feature found in so many of the promotional pictures of the sprawling acreage.

Everything about moving back to Ohio finds a way to fill me with nostalgia. The pang of a loss I shouldn't feel because I left after school somehow always working its way into my chest. It's normal to leave your college town once you've graduated. So why do I constantly feel like this?

Forcing my wayward thoughts into the recesses of my mind, I once again rake my gaze over the vibrant party around me.

Stay present, Lee. Just have fun.

Most smile as I make my way through the crowd toward the bar. A long, plain structure that covers most of the rear wall. All straight edges and lack of design. Its wood surface bland if not for the artistic decorations of cut-out hearts and dangling rose petals to hide it.

I promised Allie I would give it an hour. I'm nothing if not a woman of my word, so I make a mad dash for the bar. A drink or five is definitely necessary for me to get through this. I've been able to use the excuse of grieving for so long that jumping back into a social setting only drives my anxiety sky-high. Clammy palms, ragged breaths, thick rivulets of sweat down my spine, shifty eyes—the works.

Slipping onto one of the swanky stools, I flag the bartender. His crooked grin quirks as he holds up a single finger, pausing his flirtations with a blonde woman at the opposite end of the bar.

"What'll it be?" he stops in front of me, leaning his elbow on the edge, tapping his fingers to the beat. Flashing a megawatt smile that only makes me cringe, he tosses in a playful wink.

Too happy. Too many teeth. Way *too friendly.*

"Old fashioned, please."

"Okay. Okay. I like it," he rolls his shoulders, moving to the beat, turning away from me to get to work.

His voice carries back to me as he belts out every word of the song playing. The side-to-side bob of his head remains on beat, despite his off-key notes.

Spinning on the stool, I angle my body just enough to watch the crowd once more. An entire area has clustered near the front now. Attendees dance with arms high in the air, their joy bleeding into the space around them. I'd expected it to be a big hook-up fest, but it seems like people are genuinely trying to meet others. Form friendships, maybe dance, and just have a little fun.

I don't know. I'm not great at keeping up with my own friends. Somehow, those relationships have survived. The catch-ups lack the awkwardness I would expect to accompany the long stretches of time between calls, texts, and social media posts. Instead, it's as if we never went months without communicating.

"Here you go."

I spin back, yanking my card out of my clutch.

"No need," the bartender says. "Open bar tonight." Then he taps the surface again, returning to the blonde he'd left waiting. Swiping some cash from my wallet, I shove it into the pink mason jar I assume is for tips.

Choosing to stay put on the stool, I people-watch while sipping my drink. The repeated glances down at my phone every five minutes to track how long I've been here keep me from noticing the woman bee-lining for me. My head cocking forward, eyes squinting at her face when I finally look up again.

"Romey?" I squeak.

Her arms extend as she does that awkward run thing we women do in heels when we're excited and attempting to move quickly in a dress that likely leaves us no breathing room. The shuffle-stomp of her pumps on the slick floors seems amplified the closer she gets to me. Slipping off the stool, I open my arms to her too. "My goodness, Leighton, it's been what, a decade?"

"At least."

Holding me at arm's length, her eyes rake down my body. One that's a bit more full than the last time we saw each other in person. "You look phenomenal, but I didn't know you moved back."

"Uh, yeah. A few weeks ago, actually. Do you remember my friend Allie?"

"How could I forget? She hated that you had friends other than her." Her laughter is that same soft cackle I've memorized, but it still makes me want to flinch away from her comment.

I try not to wince at the dig. There had been a rough patch for Allie and me sophomore year when I chose to live in the dorms again. She moved off campus, and I took to volunteering and joined an academic fraternity. It took us away from each other, our friendship barely surviving on the thinnest of strings. But by that summer, when we took a lake trip with our floor mates from freshman year, we were us again.

Then I realize Romey shouldn't be at a singles gathering. I attended her freaking wedding. "Wait. Why are you here?"

She holds up her hand, showing a ringless finger, the indent still prominent. A constant reminder, I'm sure, of what she once had. "Brandon and I divorced last year."

"I'm sorry. I—" As if my memories are insistent on making a grand appearance, I recall the missed calls from her. The ones I never returned because I was still lost in my grief over Mom and working more than ever to distract myself.

She waves me off. "It happens. But you never told me why you're here."

"I moved next door to Allie. Just needed a new start."

Sadness coats her stare, but she doesn't push for information. "Well, I'm glad to see you again. Please come and meet some of my friends."

"Oh. Okay." She grabs hold of my hand, nearly making me spill my drink, but I follow her to the opposite side of the space, where a group of five women sit nestled on the couches. Each one is more gorgeous than the last. A reminder that leggings and scrubs shouldn't be my only attire. Might not hurt to visit the spa once in a while, either.

"Ladies, this is one of my fraternity sisters from college, Leighton Bergemont. Leighton, these are the ladies. Cynthia, Morgan, Erin, Ziva, and Jen." Each wave as Romey recites their names, welcoming smiles on their faces.

"Sit," Erin—I think—gestures. So I do. "Tell us about yourself," she grins widely. Her large teeth are the star feature of her face, a match for American-girl-next-door looks and golden brown wavy locks that seem to shimmer in the warm lighting.

As if my vocal cords were just waiting for someone to tell my life story to, the words tumble free. Everything from my career and why I moved here to my darling nieces. I skirt around the details of my parent's deaths, not wanting to open the floodgates of my emotions in front of strangers at a party. Fortunately, they don't press. Our conversation quickly drifting to the good old years of college and the dreads of dating in our thirties.

I'm unsure how much time has passed sitting here laughing and drinking with these women. They are the epitome of boss bitches. Lawyer, professional athlete, CEO, pediatrician, chemical engineer, and entrepreneur. The conversation flows so easily that it's almost as if I always knew them. Even the connection with Romey seems as it always was. We'd been close until she graduated a year ahead of me.

"You guys are awesome," I chuckle. "I think I'm going to head out, though. It's been a very long work week."

"Wait. Make sure we have your number. We'd love to have you come to our Sunday brunches," Morgan chirps, the first to pull out her phone, eagerly waiting for the texts to start flying as I relay my number to Romey.

Only seconds later, each woman's phone lights up with my information. "Spell your name for me," Jen grumbles. They all laugh.

"She might be the best criminal defense lawyer around, but the woman can't spell a damn thing," Cynthia deadpans. Her monotone voice only adds to the humor of the moment. My own laughter mixing with theirs. It's not the first time I've been asked to spell my name, and it won't be the last.

Romey only snatches Jen's phone, entering it for her, before tossing it back into her friend's lap.

"It was so nice meeting all of you," I wave behind me before my front collides with a solid wall of muscle.

Swallowing hard, my eyes trail up over the broad chest and shoulders into the most piercing blue eyes I've ever seen.

Holy mother of all things...

Chapter 6

GAVIN

Wide deep amber eyes stare up at me. Petite palms up and facing me as if trying to keep her balance. I'd seen the heels she was wearing. It wouldn't be hard to fall over. Hell, I've watched Ember stumble, trip, and nearly break an ankle for years now.

"Are you okay?" I ask, grabbing hold of her arm when she begins to lean to the right. Her wide eyes stay locked on me as if frozen in place, unable to blink or shift direction. "Hello?" My brow furrows low, wondering if she's deaf or drunk.

No, not deaf. I'd just seen her talking to those women in the corner.

"Yeah. Good." My eyes immediately shoot down to her full lips as she presses them together hard, forcing a swallow. The bob along her slender, elegant neck drawing my gaze downward before I drag it back up, only stalling at her pouty mouth for a split second.

She shifts her arm out of my grip and takes a step back. Her big brown eyes, which appear as large saucers, focus on my face. The minuscule movement of her gaze rakes over my features, which is as unnerving as it is intriguing.

I wonder what she sees.

Someone of interest or just a large man in her way?

Ducking down, bringing our faces level, her sweet floral scent hits me. My nose twitching as I fight not to take a long inhale like some weird psycho. Something like disappointment settling in my chest when she suddenly averts her gaze. "You sure?"

Nodding slowly, she clutches her purse to her stomach.

Only then do I unfold back to my full height. Almost six and a half feet of it. Another gift from Dad.

I don't know what else to say. She's not walking away, and for some reason, I don't want to either. There's something in her stare that seems so familiar. An emotion I can't quite place but know I should be able to. One I believe I constantly walk the edge of.

"Look, uh. I'm sorry for running into you. Can I get you a drink?" My fingers automatically reach for her again before letting my hand drop beside my thigh.

I don't know this woman. There's not a single reason in this world I should want to feel her skin beneath my palms again. Or inhale that intoxicating scent that seems to ooze out of her pores.

Her nose scrunches, eyes darting to the side, then back to mine as if confused. "It's an open bar."

Right, I knew that. It's one of the perks my sister and her friends were so proud of pulling off for several of their events. Apparently, it's difficult to get these venues to include conveniences such as food and drink for reasonable prices.

"Right. You're right."

"Um, yeah."

Fuck, I've never been this awkward with anyone in my life. And she's still just standing here. With that dress hugging her curves and her glowing skin and sparkling brown eyes.

Calm down, Gavin!

"How about a drink somewhere else, then?" I try, taking a step closer to her.

Fuck. Fuck. Fuck. She's going to think I'm asking her on a date.

Am I asking her on a date?

"I was actually, uh, heading... out." She points her thumb toward the entrance. Yet her body angles my way as if in invitation.

"Oh, yeah. Me too. Um, I can walk you to your car."

Why am I so fucking insistent on not walking away from her? She seems fine. I have a solid enough build, but she shouldn't have a concussion from colliding with my chest. It's not her well-being that keeps my dress shoes glued to the floor beneath me, though.

So what is it?

"I didn't drive."

"Oh. I can walk you outside or drive you home, then."

She only stares at me quizzically. Her fingers toying with the clasp of her purse, my jaw working in response. But she doesn't say anything. Her teeth sink into her bottom lip, the corner of her pouty mouth twitching as if wanting to quirk high.

"I'm being super creepy, aren't I?"

Ready to walk away and stop embarrassing myself in front of this gorgeous woman, her giggle keeps me rooted in place. The soft tenor serves as an anchor securing my feet where I stand.

"Yeah, you're being a little creepy. But maybe another drink would be good."

A crooked grin spreads across my face, bending my elbow so she can take it.

Lightning streaks down my spine at the feel of her looping her arm through mine. My pulse kicks into high gear as her scent envelopes me, and her fingers softly brush over the exposed skin at my wrist.

Leading her to the front of the bar, we both hand our tickets to the guy working the coat room. He finds them in record time. An unheard-of mercy at events like these.

Keeping my attention on the woman beside me, I help her slip into her sleeves, my fingers skimming across her skin. My need to touch her unforgiving, odd, and consuming.

"Thanks," she says with a shy smile, biting her lip and training her focus on her feet.

"Of course. Are you okay to walk in those?"

Sparkling eyes meet mine before casting back down to her shoes as if just remembering she's wearing sparkly gold stilettos. Shoes Ember would call, "Fuck Me Heels."

"How far are we talking?"

"A block."

She shrugs, tucking a curl behind her ear, exposing the soft curve of her jaw. "Let's find out."

I hadn't even given her my elbow again, but she slips her hand around my arm, pressing in close to my side. When I don't move, she only looks up at me before noticing I'm staring at where she holds onto me. A simple tangle of arms that can mean nothing and everything.

"Oh, sorry," she begins to pull her hand free. "I didn't think—" She puffs out a heavy breath. "Just extra balance, ya know."

"It's fine."

With a nod, we take off down the sidewalk.

The air is absolutely frigid. I don't know how the hell she's out here in a dress like that, her coat just long enough to cover her ass but leave the stretch of her legs exposed.

I'd told her a drink, but in truth, I was starving, and maybe I just didn't want to eat alone. Not tonight. Not on Valentine's Day.

My favorite steakhouse happens to be down the street, so that's where I lead us, guiding her inside just as fresh snowflakes begin to fall.

That cock-stirring giggle escapes her again as she dusts the tiny white clumps from her hair and my shoulder. "I forgot how cold it is here in the winter." Her violent shiver vibrating from her through my body.

"Let me." My fingers curl along the inside collar of her coat, slowly slipping it off her shoulders and down her arms. Those amber eyes watch me over her shoulder, lips parting as my fingers once again purposely trail over the bare skin of her arms.

"Such a gentleman." The words are playful as she slips into her seat.

Sliding into the booth across from her, she looks different in this light. More breathtaking, if that's possible. "Did you move away for a while or something?" I ask while a waiter fills our water glasses.

"Yeah," she looks down with a small laugh before catching my gaze again. "I went to school at OSU, then went home to New York until a few weeks ago." She gives one of those closed-lipped smiles as if it means nothing. Maybe it isn't to her, but most of us who choose to leave this area don't come back. There has to be a good reason, and I'm suddenly very curious about it.

"That's funny. I went to school there too."

A wide grin breaks across her face, showcasing perfect teeth. Her eyes scrunched enough it looks like she's squinting. The pure joy of a shared connection shining brightly in the way she holds her body just a fraction closer to the edge of the table. "No way. What year?"

"Graduated '08."

"Wow. Small world. I was '09."

"That's crazy. I mean, I know the school is huge, but I'm sure I never ran into you."

Her teeth sink into her bottom lip again, eyes casting downward before pulling her water glass in front of her. A line of moisture follows it, but she pays it no mind. "I'm not surprised. I lived in the towers when I was a freshman and then in Drackett sophomore year before moving into my fraternity house junior and senior year."

My palm cracks against the tabletop, disbelief leaving my mouth gaping wide. The world is simultaneously too large and too small. "I had a bunch of friends in Morrill. A handful of the football guys lived there sophomore year."

"I know. We had a suite of them next door."

My eyes go wide. Had I just never noticed her? Does she look different now than she did then?

"Small world," I echo her sentiment just as our waitress returns.

"What are you having?" Dragging a black leather book and pen from her apron pocket, her high-pitched voice momentarily steals my attention.

I turn my gaze to the woman in front of me, realizing I still haven't asked her name. "Eight-ounce filet, medium, no asparagus, extra mashed potatoes." She hands over the menu she never even cracked open.

"Same," I choke, too frazzled to order something healthier the way I normally would.

"My parents used to love this place when they would come to visit. I'm surprised it's still here." She glances down at her hands, her eyes fluttering shut for a moment before she looks back up at me.

"Are you okay?"

She winces, setting her hands atop the table, her fingers dragging over one another. "Honestly, no. My best friend insisted I come out tonight, so I wasn't alone on Valentine's Day. Truthfully, I would have preferred to stay home with my nieces, mourning my parents. But she says I need to get out more because I've become too comfortable being alone."

Those warm brown eyes meet mine, filled with embarrassment she has no need to feel.

"You didn't want to hear all that," she flicks her hand, shaking her head, those loose curls forming a curtain around her face. "I think I should get home."

But my hand cups over hers, holding her in place. "My sister didn't want me to be alone tonight, either. Apparently, she's tired of watching me mope."

I'm not sure why I am so drawn to this woman, but I don't want her to be alone. At least for tonight, neither one of us needs to be.

"Please stay."

She settles back in her seat. "On one condition."

"Name it." The pitch of my voice is more eager than it should be. But something tells me if this woman walks away, I'll never see her again, and I can't have that either.

"We talk about anything other than why our loved ones thought we were so lonely we needed to go to a singles meet and greet tonight."

A barked laugh escapes me, my head flying back before I meet her gaze again.

"Done. That's the easiest thing a woman has ever asked of me."

Chapter 7

LEIGHTON

I CAN'T REMEMBER THE last time I laughed so much.

It's interesting how clear a picture becomes in retrospect. The happy lives we thought we were leading turned out to be the opposite when we experienced things we thought we had. I thought I'd been somewhat happy and enjoyed those I did spend time with.

I didn't.

I wasn't.

As my hand cups my mouth for what must be the millionth time in an effort to stifle my laughter since meeting this man, I can't help but reflect. When was the last time I genuinely enjoyed someone's company outside of the few friends I did still see?

When did I last allow myself to breathe?

This man was not what I expected. From the well-fitted suit and the exotic looks, I didn't think I'd stand more than five minutes in his company. Forget holding any sort of conversation, whether intellectual or amusing;

I didn't think I'd want any of it with the cold blue eyes sitting across from me. Eyes that are truthfully so much warmer than they appear.

His laughter suddenly stops, gaze roving over the now empty restaurant. "I think we might be holding them up."

I hadn't even noticed the place had emptied. The servers have already cleaned and set the tables for tomorrow. Glancing down at my watch, it's just before midnight. Almost four hours of sitting with this handsome man seemed to pass in the blink of an eye. How do things like that happen?

We're quick to make our way outside, the frigid night air immediately working its way into my body. My entire frame shivering to stave off what feels like instant frostbite after hours immersed in the toasty warm interior of the restaurant.

"Come here," he whispers, his own teeth chattering as he drapes an arm around my shoulders. Long fingers flex against my arm, pulling me into his side. The masculine scent of his cologne making me want to settle in even closer.

As if he could read my mind, he crushes me against his hard body. We might as well be glued together, walking in perfect rhythm like two lovers on a night stroll. He smells like Christmas and bad decisions, distracting me, but his warmth somehow reaches me even through our thick coats.

"Can I drive you home? I would rather not let you catch a ride this late at night alone."

My eyes meet his. The coloring is suddenly more vibrant despite the dim lighting. Those captivating irises bracketed by creases of concern around his eyes. A sign he must always be like this with people. "You don't have to go out of your way to do that."

"I promise I'm not a creep or anything. I just want to make sure you get home safely."

How do I tell him it has nothing to do with that? Somehow, I feel completely comfortable with him. Like our souls have known each other forever, but it's only been four hours.

Four hours of not feeling so alone. Four hours of companionship I'd failed to realize I'd been missing in my life.

What I don't want to tell him is I don't know how to let people take care of me outside of Allie and my parents. Allie will tell you even they aren't the exception. She's constantly fighting me tooth and nail to do anything for me. It was a problem I had in past relationships, too.

I'm the poster child for little miss do-it-herself. I'm just not good at accepting help.

"Really? I'm a big girl. I'll be fine."

His face hovers mere centimeters over mine, those crystalline blue eyes trailing to my mouth before meeting my stare once more. There's no stopping the parting of my lips or my increased respiration, my teeth sinking into my bottom lip as his gaze bores into me.

"Please."

The single word sends his warm breath fanning over my face. Holy hell, if I don't feel that single word in places that I shouldn't. Places that have been dormant for some time now.

"Yeah. Okay." What was meant to be the same quiet acceptance I often give Allie comes out breathy. Embarrassing enough, pleading for him to escort me home would be less humiliating.

He only smiles. Big and broad, showcasing his teeth and those deep creases at the corners of his eyes.

Dropping his arm, he grabs hold of my hand with a soft tug, signaling me to follow him.

Luckily, we only have to walk about twenty feet. A sparkling black SUV sits parked right on the corner of where the gathering had been. How his vehicle is clean through all this murky water and slush is beyond me. Only a small spray line lingers along the bottom.

Thumping music draws my attention to the right. The party is still in full swing, with several people entering despite the time. Their laughter hits me as if I were standing right next to them, causing me to shake my head.

Couldn't be me. Those college days of getting to parties after eleven p.m. are long over.

A hand softly rests against the small of my back, drawing my attention up to my... date? With a crooked grin, he leads me to the passenger side, opening the door for me. "Thank you," I whisper.

I expect him to close my door as soon as I'm in my seat, but he simply stands there, fingers curled around the edge of the frame.

His gaze trails to the seatbelt before locking with mine again. I recognize this move from my books, so I quickly pull the strap across my body before settling into the buttery, soft leather. Only a small, uncharacterizable sound comes from him, drawing my focus back to his face. His wide, crooked grin greets me before he nods.

My mind automatically wanders, imagining he'd thrown in a "good girl."

The muscles in my lower belly clench, my thighs pressing together instantly.

Why was that so damn hot?

Lost in the fantasies of what would come next after a moment like that in my romance novels, I don't notice him climb into the driver's seat beside me. The car purrs to life, his long fingers tapping buttons on the screen before the air starts blowing through the vents. "Your seat warmer buttons are there. I turned them all the way up, but if it gets too hot—"

"Are you kidding me? Having a toasty ass is my favorite thing."

He only stares at me with a cocked brow. I'd meant those words to sound more like a joke, though I am dead serious. My only success here is sounding like a crazy person. A fact clear by his bewildered expression. Now would be a great time to crawl in a hole and never come out.

Yet, my gut assures me I don't need to hide my weirdness from him. Liking seat warmers is a totally normal thing. Except in the dead of summer, mine stays on. Allie hates it, but my car, my rules.

Then I'm second-guessing myself. His stare seems more intense, and his expression hasn't changed. *Dammit, this is why I avoid people.* "Uh, well. Okay. Sorry."

"Don't apologize," he grunts, tapping the screen again. "What's your address?"

I give it to him, and he pulls out onto the road without another word.

We travel the still-busy streets in silence. One that's as uncomfortable as it feels natural.

Watching Columbus zoom by outside my window brings back a harsh wave of memories. I'd spent four years here. Years I'd almost extended, then chickened out, thinking I was homesick. I was, but I wasn't.

I was scared.

It was normal to be away from my parents during college, but it felt like I was abandoning them to not return home. Maybe, in a way, I'd done the right thing. It gave me a safe place to land when school took me down a different path, and I was there for both of their deaths.

But now I wonder "what if."

For months, I cried and moped about missing Columbus. It was my constant for four years, including three summers between academic years. Though I never told my parents, a piece of my heart was broken when I left.

Hot tears burn behind my eyes and nose, and then his palm finds my thigh. The soft squeeze pulling me out of the dark path my thoughts were happily ready to River Dance down. An opportunity for the grief to pull me under. A perfect way to end a surprisingly great night. "Do you like music?"

I can only nod. "Use your words. If I watch you instead of the road, we're not making it back to your house tonight."

I swallow hard. Where did this guy come from? Who talks like that?

Lee, you know the answer. Men in your filthy books do.

"Yeah. I'll listen to anything, but I'm a sucker for an unrequited love song."

He shifts in his seat again, lifting his hand from my thigh long enough to tap the screen once more before settling against the bit of fabric just above where my bare skin pokes free. The weight of his palm seems to bring my body alive, while the soft hum just beneath the surface keeps me conscious of his touch.

Adele's husky voice floats through the speakers. Her lyrics heartbreaking and haunting all at once. I hum along to the beat, forcing myself to stare out the window instead of the handsome man beside me.

I'm once again lost in my thoughts when I realize I don't even know his name. How could I have not asked?

The moment my mouth opens to do just that, he pulls into my short driveway. The car easing to a smooth stop just in front of my garage.

He shifts the car into park but doesn't move otherwise. Sitting straight, his focus lingers somewhere outside the windshield. Whether it's my house occupying him or nothing at all isn't clear. Not with his blank stare that gives away nothing. I watch his Adam's apple bob at his throat, wondering if he's going to say anything or if he's just waiting for me to get out of the car so he can go about his night and be free of the weirdo.

"Um, thanks for the ride."

I'm fumbling to undo my seatbelt, and reaching for my door, just cracking it open when he speaks again. "Hold on. Close it."

I pause, wondering if I made a grave mistake about this man. Maybe he's one of those fascinating serial killers who lures women with their charm, and this is the moment he's going to kill me and put me inside my house as if that's where he committed the crime.

My pulse races. Each swallow is like passing a lump of coal down my throat. The painful sting making me wince each time.

Paralysis seems to take over my body. The muscles won't move, even though I'm pleading for them to in my mind. I need to run or defend myself, but can only stay right where I am, holding the door cracked open.

As if terrified, he jumps from the driver's seat, jogging around to my side. When he softly closes my door, I flinch. My body unclenches only to spasm back into a tense hold. My musculoskeletal system fighting to jerk back to life, ready to climb over the middle consul if he tries anything untoward.

Shit. Shit. Shit. The single word a chant in my mind as if it will do something to help me when Mr. Sexy and Charming tries to strangle me with his bare hands.

When he opens the door again, there's a look in his eyes I can't quite place. Worry. An apology. I'm not entirely sure. "I, uh, just wanted to open your door for you."

For the millionth time tonight, I just sit there and stare at him. My hands shake when I take his as he helps me out of the SUV. He doesn't release me, instead weaving his fingers through mine, leading us to my front door. His silence and the tension in his upper body speak volumes, and suddenly, I feel like an idiot.

I'd made a horrible assumption, but can you blame a girl? It wouldn't be the first time a female fell for a man's looks and ended up dead.

As if trying to ensure I have a witness or backup, my gaze drifts to Allie's house. Except for the side door lamp, which casts a soft glow across the grass, all the lights are out. Their family is sound asleep, tucked into bed.

It's no surprise, they're all half-unconscious by nine most nights. So weird.

"Thank you for having dinner with me," he says as we stop at my front door. The sconce lights seem to illuminate his features: his icy eyes, his full bottom lip, and the wisps of gray scattered throughout his dark beard.

That salt in pepper causes my teeth to sink into my bottom lip again. I've always been a sucker for the look.

"Thank you for dinner." A soft smile curves my lips. My chuckle causing him to quirk a brow. "Allie said I would have a great time tonight if I let myself."

His hand finds my waist, the softest tug pulling me closer to him. Piercing eyes search mine before drifting down to my mouth. A tell I've watched him do several times tonight.

"I'm glad you had fun with me." His fingers flex, my body tingling all over again. The press of my thighs failing to staunch the ache that's been gradually building.

"Did you have fun..." my question stalls.

"Gavin." He steps closer, his face angling down toward mine. "Gavin Norwood."

My hands find his upper arms, staring up into those eyes that I can't seem to look away from. He pulls me an inch closer, our bodies flush, his large palm flat against my hip while the other still squeezes my waist.

"Nice to meet you." The words are nothing more than whispy breaths as I watch his eyes find my mouth again. "Thank you... again... for..."

I can't seem to get the words out as he dips his face closer to mine. So close our mouths will brush if one of us speaks. The muscles down below clenching in anticipation of a kiss we both seem to want. It's been a long time. I'm supposed to embrace this, right?

"We should get you inside." His words are measured as he presses in tight against me. The brush of those soft lips over mine is feather-light but still undoubtedly sets my insides on fire. My internal temperature so high I forget we're standing out in the freezing cold.

"Yeah, we should."

"Unlock the door. Go inside." Then he backs away, putting a sliver of space between us.

I'm instantly plunged back into ice-capped depths, though his fingers still flex at my waist.

"Yeah, okay." Digging in my clutch, I yank my keys free. Eager to break all contact, I flush with embarrassment. Facing him again, I keep my hands on the door and the frame. "Thank you again. It was fun."

Feeling like I did something wrong and trying to shut Gavin Norwood out, I move to secure the only barrier I have between us. The groan of the hinges overshadowed by his gruff voice.

"Wait!" His palm meets the solid wood, keeping it from closing. "What's your name?"

"Leighton."

Chapter 8

GAVIN

It's been three days since I met Leighton. I haven't stopped thinking about her for a single second. Especially that look in her eyes when she thought I was going to kiss her.

I was going to. Only not knowing her name stopped me. I wanted to know who was about to ruin me with those pouty lips.

But the moment she told me her name, she closed the door in my face, the click of the lock seconds later confirming the night was over. I'd thought about knocking. You know that shit they do in movies when he's standing on the other side of the door, breathing heavily before he crashes into her?

Then the visions of how panicked she'd become when I told her to shut the door slammed into me. A reminder that I should have opened my damn mouth instead of pulling some sort of I'm-a-manly-man shit. It didn't matter how many wonderful hours we spent together; I was still a stranger. One whose name she didn't even know at the time.

Knowing I'd unintentionally scared her shook me to my core, and I just couldn't beg her to open that door again.

I've chastised myself these past few days for how weird and creepy I'd been. No wonder she didn't want to see me again. At least, that's my assumption when she left me out there in the cold.

A reality I'll have to deal with unless I randomly run into her around Columbus.

This is the only opportunity I might ever have to plead my case and maybe convince her to go on a proper date with me.

Though there's no doubt in my mind, Valentine's Day counts as our first.

I was so caught up in our dinner conversation that I didn't even think to ask for her number.

Connections like that don't happen every day.

It's the type where you lose track of time and purpose. It's just you and that person vibing on a level that sometimes seems unattainable. Not when everything is digital, and we all live on our phones 24/7.

The vibration of my phone against the desk pulls me back into the present.

Craig: Pick up your phone!

Shit. I'd forgotten my best buddy from college was coming in next week. Our annual cabin getaway. Over the years, we've had to find somewhere bigger to rent as my friends have found their significant others and brought them along.

And for the fifth year in a row, I'm stuck going alone.

It doesn't matter how many women I've attempted to date since Jen. They either haven't lasted long enough for one of our quarterly trips, or I simply didn't want to invite them. That fact alone foretold how I felt about a future with them.

There wasn't one.

The proven checkpoint where we always went our separate ways.

Fuck, I hate being single.

Me: I'll call you back in 5

Anything to distract me from my obsessive thoughts about a woman I may never see again.

Craig: Aww sugar you're too good to me.

A barking laugh leaves me. Craig Holleran has always been like this. His southern roots used as a way to crack jokes rather than something he actually holds any genuine fondness over.

He'd been eager to escape Alabama, coming to Ohio State on a football scholarship the same as I did. We met on the field and automatically became inseparable.

Our bromance is definitely one for the books. We used to tell people we were brothers because of our nearly matching eyes, but we never got away with it. His pale complexion—until the sun touched his skin in summer—and ash-blond hair, in contrast to my darker features, gave us away.

Nevertheless, blood or not, Craig has been my brother in all the ways that count since the day we met.

Shutting down my laptop, I snatch my phone off the desk.

> **Me: Actually I'll call you in a few hours. Have something I need to do.**

> **Craig: Fine! I'll suffer in silence while I wait for your call**

> **Me: You're such a dramatic asshole**

> **Craig: Damn straight**

I only chuckle as I disappear into my bedroom, change, and head out. If anyone might know Leighton from the party, it'll definitely be Ember.

I can only hope she'd been the one to greet her and not one of her friends.

Looks like I'm about to find out.

"Anything new?" Craig asks before taking a massive bite of his Reuben sandwich.

I prefer only being subjected to phone conversations, but he insists on video calls. Says he misses seeing my face.

In truth, I miss him too. I miss all my friends. For four years, we were all right there together. But then some of us moved away, and adulthood took up our time. Even years later, it seems like I am sometimes still adjusting to not seeing them every day.

I stall for a moment, wondering if I should tell him about Leighton or not.

Taking Ember to lunch to pump her for information had proven to be a bust. She couldn't even recall seeing a woman there that looked like Leighton. My mind starting to wonder if I imagined her.

Only I remember what it felt like to touch her. Every memory of her giggle in my head makes my dick twitch. The cadence of her quickened breaths over my face as we stood outside her house in the cold haunts my dreams.

She was real.

She was there.

I've been trying to figure out a way to see her again. A plan that doesn't revolve around me showing up at her house unannounced like a stalker, but I haven't come up with a damn thing.

"Who is she?" Craig grins.

Motherfucker.

There's no point in trying to lie. I'm the hopeless romantic. Anytime I meet someone I'm excited about, it's written in every part of my demeanor. The joy over her potentially being "the one" oozes out of my pores like liquor after a black-out drunken night of partying. I'm practically a flashing neon sign that says *Guys, I think I found Mrs. Norwood.* "I met her on Valentine's Day at Ember's meet-up thing."

"And?"

I shrug, poking at my salad. A bright red cherry tomato rolling away as if trying to avoid being eaten just as much as I don't want to eat it. "And I took her to dinner and then drove her home."

"And?" he presses.

"And that's it. We had a great time. I didn't get her number." I shovel a forkful of lettuce into my mouth. The greens do nothing to appease me. I try to eat healthy as much as possible, but honestly, I hate it. I would prefer french fries and cakes.

"That's. It?" Craig swallows loudly. Wide eyes meet mine as his mouth falls open.

"Not all of us try to get into a woman's pants after five minutes."

"That's rude," he points a finger my way. "I wait at least thirty."

Craig isn't shy about being a ladies' man. He doesn't do relationships. Sleeps around as much as he likes. The women know the score when they meet him. He never pretends it's anything more than that. We all wish he would settle down, but know why he doesn't.

The divorce between his parents when he was ten hit him hard. He'd witnessed every fight. Every nasty slung word and how his parents took jabs at each other for no other reason than it hurt like hell.

That type of petty abuse sticks with you no matter how you try to forget or what type of person it molds you into.

What makes it worse is that he remembers the good years, too—the ones filled with love before hard times hit. Money, or the lack thereof, makes it easy for people to tear each other apart. Stress and frustrations can become impossible to put on the back burner instead of focusing on the partnership.

His parents failed to put each other first, and everything they once had crumbled.

"Anyway," I roll my eyes, chomping on another forkful of the tasteless lettuce, this bite lacking a single additional ingredient.

"When are you going to see her again?"

I pause, my jaw working to chew the remnants of my food before smiling. One I couldn't stop even if I tried. Though I've not found a way yet, the prospect of experiencing her voice vibrating through my chest once more perks me up. "I just told you I don't have her number."

He shrugs. "You know where her house is, and you're romantic and shit. Send her some flowers and a card or something. Like, make it mysterious 'Meet me at the place we first met at seven p.m. Thursday.'" Craig's shoulders roll with his dramatics, but I just stare.

My best friend is fucking brilliant!

Craig doesn't have a romantic bone in his body. His idea of showing a woman "romance" is making her scream his name at least five times in a single night. But his idea sounds just crazy enough that it might work.

"Thanks for the advice," I snicker. "Tell me what's going on with you."

"Landed that new contract for that resort in Vegas. We start work in a few weeks."

"You're kidding?"

"They couldn't resist one of the best architects in the world."

I can only snort. Craig has always been like this. He acts like an arrogant ass, but he's smart as hell. Unlike me, he played football so he had a way out of his state. He worked his ass off for that scholarship, eager for a sound education at a reputable institution.

His original plan was business. A career of office life, suits, and ties would have been miserable for him. He only fell into architecture after we'd ventured to one of the libraries on North Campus one afternoon. He spent more time staring at all the lines than studying for his sociology exam. It just took off from there.

"Proud of you, man. The guys will be excited to hear it too."

His eyes shift down to the last bit of sandwich on his plate. His long fingers poking at it. "Thanks."

For a man who walks around with his chin cocked high and an ego the size of an elephant, he's very different when it comes to his career. That arrogance fades away anytime we show genuine pride over what he has accomplished.

It makes me wonder if his family still gives him a hard time about moving to a fancy city and never looking back. A topic of contention we've slugged through countless times over the years. He should never let their harsh words devalue what he has accomplished, but none of us are perfect at fighting our demons.

We finish up our dinner in silence before I end the call, promising to catch up with him later.

As I place my phone face down on my desk, I know I should get back to work. I accomplished little earlier today, and I have a million deadlines looming with high-profile clients right around the corner—clients who should have all of my undivided attention.

But my memories steal my focus. So many flit through my mind. Twenty years with my best friends has left me with plenty of them. So, shutting my work laptop, I go in search of my personal one.

The moment I settle in on my couch, laptop open, I head to my social media page. There are hundreds of albums here, grouped into these moments that meant everything at the time. Every memory through college and so many more since always at my fingertips.

Clicking on an album from sophomore year, a smile curves across my face. Student night at the Columbus Zoo was crazy. Hundreds of us went that night, running through the exhibits, laughing, and scarfing down junk food. Fortunately, there weren't very many visitors there because most of us acted like drunken fools—too many of us actually were.

The thumbnails fill the screen. The digital camera we took these on is still tucked in a bin somewhere in the back of my closet. A gadget I refused to get rid of because it captured every single one of these moments and froze them in time for us.

Clicking on the first one, a laugh bursts free.

I remember the moment perfectly. The guys and I had our arms linked over each other's shoulders as we laughed like we didn't have a care in the world. Reed, Craig, then me, Ace, Tyler, Kian, and lastly, Nick. The seven of us have been friends since our freshman year. A friendship that has only grown stronger over the years. Though only Reed, Tyler, and I still live in Ohio, we all make a point to see each other quarterly, if not more. No exceptions.

Even when Reed had his ACL repaired and was in a brace and on crutches, he hobbled his ass down to Mexico for our summer beach tour. No doubt we're all getting struck by lightning someday for how much we laughed at him instead of helping him traipse over the sand.

Continuing to scroll through the pictures, I stop on another one of us. I've got Reed cradled in my arms and Craig on my back. What looks like the lion's cage looms behind me. But that's not what snags my attention. It's the two women hugging and laughing in the background. Lowering my face to the screen as if that will zoom in on the picture, my eyes grow wide.

It's her.

It's Leighton. Her hair had been much shorter then, just past her shoulder blades with a soft wave to it. Her frame is much thinner than it is now, but there's no mistaking the straight nose with the bulb at the end and her high cheekbones.

How had I never noticed her before?

And suddenly I know what to do so I can see her again.

I can only hope she'll show.

Chapter 9

LEIGHTON

"There are my favorite girls!" My arms fly open as I step into Allie's kitchen, ready to catch my nieces.

They jump at me in unison, their feet dangling mid-air as I stand up straight. I would think Abby would have grown out of this phase by now, but she hasn't. At least not with me. She'd probably ask me to carry her around the store like a baby if she thought I'd agree.

"Soon, I won't be able to pick you guys up anymore."

"Then you just have to get stronger, Auntie Lee," Tori giggles before leaping down and sprinting into the next room. As if automated, my eyes roll, listening to the slap of her bare feet against the hardwood floors.

She used to refuse to take off her socks, resulting in several slips and falls that ended in tears and tubs of ice cream. Eventually, Allie banned her from wearing socks around the house, even in the winter. *"Your Auntie Lee needs a break from checking for broken bones,"* she scolded her daughter, always with that playful hint of humor in her Caribbean blue eyes.

"Allie," I call louder than necessary when she suddenly pops her head up over the edge of the island opposite where I stand.

Per usual, she looks frazzled. Her dirty brown hair twisted in a messy knot atop her head, and not a stitch of makeup on her face. If she's not going to the office, this is her typical. A baseline, if you will.

She groans loudly, pushing to her feet. "I swear these kids will be the death of me. Please take them."

"Don't tempt me with a good time," I chuckle.

"Girls, pack your stuff!" Allie shouts. "You're going to live with your aunt."

A chorus of cheers sounds from the den before Tori comes into view, racing back into the kitchen with a basket. Her panting breaths are so loud that they drown out the slap of skin against the floor.

The clear plastic wrap reveals everything inside: chocolates, cookies, bottles of wine, a single red rose, spa items, and a card. At first glance, it's clear this was put together by hand and thought went into the contents instead of those store-bought baskets so many of us gift people we barely tolerate at the holidays.

I'm as guilty as anyone else when it comes to it. The reason I realize this is not that.

"What's this?" I ask, crouching to take a closer look. Tori's back arches as she fights to keep hold of the massive thing, but she shrugs, shoving it into my hands before running off again. The tune of another pop song drifting out behind her as she bolts up the stairs.

"I saw some guy pull into your driveway and leave that at your front door. Didn't want to leave it out there since it might rain again," Allie huffs pulling several glasses from the cabinet and a massive bottle of wine from the fridge and sitting it beside her bottle of pinot noir.

"You're too good to me." I side-hug my best friend before accepting a generous glass of wine from her and joining her in the den. Just another girl's night. One I need more than I care to admit.

Once we're settled in under our favorite Sherpa blankets, she asks, "Are you going to open it?"

I shrug, staring at the basket nestled in my lap. I hadn't even realized I refused to let it go. As if my subconscious knew it was something precious to keep close to me.

Placing my glass on the coffee table, I unabashedly tear into the plastic and reach for the card first. My teeth sink into my lower lip as I read the signature, then rake over the words above it.

Leighton (I hope I spelled that right),

I had so much fun with you the other night. More fun than I've had in ages. I haven't stopped thinking about you, and I want to see you again. No, I need *to see you again.*
Meet me at the Columbus Zoo tonight at 7 p.m.
Please don't say no.
Dress warm!

Yours,
Gavin

I read it three more times before Allie snatches the card from my fingertips.

"Who is Gavin?"

Shit. I hadn't told Allie about the man I'd met, which is shocking since I've been thinking about him nonstop.

Vivid images of him have kept me so distracted that I've been caught staring off into space, consumed by his memory. His scent and the warmth of his fingers are alive in my mind at every turn. Even my dreams are filled with Gavin Norwood and all the things I wish he had done to me that night.

Snatching my card back, I clutch it to my chest. "I met him at the V-Day party."

"And you were going to tell me when?"

I groan. I should have expected this. There is no keeping secrets from Allie. "I—It's been a long week."

"Well, you're off for two days now, so spill. Or do I need to make you take shots to talk?"

I groan again, remembering the last time Allie and I took countless shots while having girl talk. I was puking for hours. Each wretch left my throat a raw, burning mess. "No thanks," I wince. "Um, I ran into him as I was leaving, and then we went to dinner. He was so funny and charming, and fuck, his eyes make my panties wet."

"TMI, but continue." She raises her glass before taking a long pull of her red wine, the legs dancing along the edge of the glass as if waiting for my answer, too.

"I mean, that's really it. We had a great time. He drove me home and was such a gentleman, and then he left."

"Lee! You didn't even get any?"

I throw her a wry look that only makes her quirk a brow. Her challenge for me to come up with some lame excuse for why I didn't let a handsome man into my bed. "I was trying to ensure you and Mike got to do that, but you wanted me to go out."

Allie ignores my pout the way she often does.

"No need. The—"

Her words stop abruptly before she takes an uncomfortably large gulp from her glass. Her teeth bared, sucking in a deep breath.

"Allison Richards, you better not be pregnant and drinking that gallon of wine."

"I'm not... yet, but we're trying." Allie isn't the quiet type, but her voice is so low as she reveals her confession I question what this is doing to her.

Yet it doesn't stop my squeal while launching myself across the couch at my best friend. They'd had such a hard time getting pregnant with their two girls. Countless miscarriages and fertility treatments nearly broke the strong woman beside me. A heartbreaking time I wasn't there to physically support her. But I am now. I'm here, and there's no way I'm missing any of it.

"Stop it." She swats at me, drinking from her glass. "Don't make a big deal. Back to the important stuff. Are you actually going to go out there in this shitty weather to meet him?"

"I think I am," I side-eye her. "Even if nothing happens, it was nice just being comfortable with someone again."

"Then chug that wine and get off my couch. Mike will drop you off." This is the Allie way. Always volunteering her husband to take me places or help me. I know Mike doesn't mind, but dammit, I can do things myself. Not to mention I don't need the reminder that the only man in my life willing to help is my best friend's husband.

"Ugh, Allie!" My head falls back to the edge of the couch, the basket nearly slipping off the cushion beside my thigh with my movement. "I don't need your husband—"

"Your brother-in-law," she corrects.

"—driving me to a... date."

"Call it due diligence or protective older brother behavior. Whatever makes you feel better."

There's no stopping my hundredth groan since I walked into the Richards household tonight, knowing I'm not going to win this. I never win these disagreements. "Fine, but I want another glass of wine before I go."

My best friend only grins at me as the two of us drain our glasses, fill them again, and empty those, too.

✶ ✶ ✶

"You'll call me for a ride home?" Mike questions as he pulls up in front of the zoo a few hours later.

"No. I will Uber home like a normal adult."

His mouth turns down, a thumb drumming against the steering wheel at an anxiety-inducing pace, and I know what's coming. "Allie will have my balls." A whine meant to entice me to show him mercy.

"Not my problem. Love you and thank you," I call, hopping out of his car.

Mike's stare seems to burn into the back of my skull, but I won't cave. It's so much easier to tell him no than Allie. As terrible as it sounds, he's just as predictable. He'll give one push before backing down when I don't relent.

Allie will rip him a new one, but that's for them to work out. There aren't strong enough words to express my love for her. Still, that affection for her doesn't change that she has no boundaries, and sometimes she needs to be reminded that they exist.

I've always tried to be as independent as possible. Maybe it was to prove to myself that I could be though my parents still coddled me. Then they died, and I had no other choice.

No one was there to ensure I ate, slept, or cleaned my house. No one knocking on my front door to force me to get fresh air or do something fun. Allie did the best she could from afar, but until I moved here, it never really took.

Now I'm learning how to accept help, and I feel like a damn baby trying to learn to walk.

I've only just chanced a look back toward where Mike had dropped me, to find Gavin waiting right there, with his arms open. A soft grin pulling at his full mouth as if expecting me to walk right into them.

I do, letting him crush me into a tight hug. A sense of calm washes over me, and I melt into his hold as if I were always meant to be there.

"I'm so glad you came."

I'm quick to step out of his hold for fear that if I didn't, I'd never let go. He feels too good. Smells too good. Looks way too good. "Me too."

My teeth sink into my bottom lip, his gaze tracking down to my mouth with his darkening stare. As if his thumb is the only part of him he's willing to allow freedom of movement, it softly presses to my bottom lip. At first, he only holds the pad there, breathing in deep as if needing to steady himself for some big moment. Then it shifts. Just the gentlest brush along my glossed mouth.

My breath hitches. This is the first time he's intentionally touched my skin. My chest pumps high, unsure what is about to happen, welcoming whatever it might be.

He pulls softly, my teeth releasing the plump flesh. "Better. For now," he adds so low I barely hear him as he holds out his arm for me to take.

My hand instantly snakes through the crook of his arm. The action seems so normal, even though I've only held him twice this very same way. Somehow, everything about Gavin and I seems so... natural.

He's already purchased our tickets, so we can walk right inside. Twinkling lights illuminate the pathways and exhibits, and it's just like I remember it.

There was a night during my freshman year when all students got free entry. The weather was still warm then. The opposite of the frigid cold lingering tonight. My shiver throwing Gavin into motion. That heavy arm draping over my shoulders the same way he'd done the night we met.

A gesture more comforting than it should be. Welcome even.

"Did you ever come for the student nights?" I ask.

"I did," he chuckles. "Actually, I want to show you something."

I only nod as he shifts his phone into my line of sight, pulling up a picture.

He's the focal point, holding up two other guys—also insanely hot—but he zooms in, showcasing the two women hugging in the background.

Holy fuck!

"How did you get this?" I breathe.

"I just noticed it the other day. I have a tendency to look at old pictures when I'm feeling nostalgic, and I happened to notice you in the background."

I shake my head, staring at the picture. I remember the moment perfectly. It was me and Allie cackling at her making roaring sounds to try to get the lion's attention. But the damn cat wouldn't come to the cage, so we just laughed, holding each other up while our stomach's burned.

"Geez, this feels like yesterday."

"I know," he tucks his phone back in his pocket, draping his arm over my shoulders again. "But I thought I would bring you here. Kind of like recreating a moment we never got to have."

Spinning in front of him, he stares down at me. *Damn, he's tall.* "I have a better idea. Instead of recreating that night, let's make a new one."

His smile lights up the night, his cold palm sliding over my cheek before he presses the softest kiss there. "Deal."

Chapter 10

GAVIN

I'VE NEVER HAD SUCH great dates back to back. My body is literally floating on cloud nine as I pull into Leighton's driveway. An essence of euphoria keeping me high on the drug that is Leighton Bergemont.

"Gavin, that was the coldest date I've ever been on, but thank you for inviting me." Her hand lightly grips my forearm, her smile shy, but I can only stare at those lips. I hadn't meant to pry her lip from her teeth earlier, and I'd damn near kissed her mouth then, but I wanted to be a gentleman too.

After scaring her that night, I needed her to trust me before making my move. A move I wasn't sure she would accept, no matter how much those brown eyes seemed to beg me for more.

"Much better than that night in the picture," I chuckle, watching her shy away from the compliment.

"Did you have dinner?" she asks, her voice quiet.

"No. Did you?"

She giggles. The sound shooting straight to my cock. The bastard twitching in my jeans wanting to hear it again. "Only if wine counts as a food group."

"Leighton," I grumble. My tone a warning. She shouldn't have been drinking or out here in the freezing cold on an empty stomach.

"We can order takeout if you want to come in. I can't cook, so that's my best offer."

I've never cut the engine and jumped out of my car so damn fast. That giggle hitting me again the moment I open her door. "So that's a yes?"

"That's a hell yes, sweetheart."

She leads me by the hand to her front door, unlocking it before ushering me inside. "Welcome to my humble abode." Her arm sweeps out to the side, a wide grin pulling at the corners of her mouth. Pride shines in her eyes. This isn't just a place she lives or keeps her stuff. This place is important to her, and I want to know why.

In truth, I want to know every damn thing about her.

Allowing my gaze to drift over her space, a coziness instantly wraps me in a tight hold. Her house is perfect—homey but modern. Pictures line the walls that aren't hidden behind bookshelves, every single one full.

"It looks new."

"I guess it is, sort of," she calls from around the corner. I'd been so busy taking in every detail that I hadn't noticed she moved out of the entryway.

I find her in the massive kitchen, rifling through a drawer as she slaps several menus on the granite countertops. Tucking a chunk of hair behind her ear, she bends low, peering into the drawer as if it's keeping secrets from her, before yanking a single pamphlet free.

Sliding up next to her, my hand finds her lower back. Thai. Chinese. American. Pizza. Mediterranean. Her collection of menus shouldn't impress me, but it does. "Want anything in particular?" I duck my head close to her ear. A shudder soaring through her body as my breath brushes her exposed skin.

"As long as there are french fries available, I don't care."

Picking up the menu that showcases burgers, wings, and fried mozzarella sticks on the front, I flip it open. Go figures they only have two types of salad: Caesar and House.

"What do you want? I'll call the order in."

"Wings. Hot. Fries. Chicken parm sandwich," she smiles up at me, the corner of her mouth quickly dropping. "What?"

"Nothing." To be clear, I love a woman who can eat, but damn, the only green food item will be celery sticks if they send them with her wings. It's been years since I've freely eaten like that, so it throws me off when other people around me do.

Pulling out my phone, she leans in close, watching me click the items in the app. My thumb tapping the screen to submit the order, only to notice her glaring at me. "A salad?"

"Yeah, why?"

"There's not even any meat on it." Her features scrunch, tone incredulous as she leans away from me.

"I like salads."

Her snort carries back to me as she angles her way toward a family room just off the kitchen. "No one likes salads, Gavin."

She's right. I hate them, but it's been harder to maintain this physique the older I get. One I'm not sure is worth hanging onto most days.

I was always playing sports. Possessing natural athletic abilities made remaining active second nature to me. Back then, it took no effort to keep in shape, but I've also always been on the thinner side. Building muscle on my frame took a lot of work, so I wasn't mistaken for the Jolly Green Giant's cousin.

Ultimately, it's not about my looks. I don't give a fuck. It's about the blood, sweat, tears, and dedication I've put into constructing my body. There's nothing I've ever worked harder at than that.

"I see you read a lot." My poor attempt at changing the subject as I settle in next to her.

A soft smile pulls at the corners of her mouth as her eyes rove over the three walls full of books. Then she's on her feet, walking over to the shelf right in front of us. Delicate fingers dance over the spines. A soft display of love for her bound bundles of paper pulling at her features.

"I used to read more, but work and life..." Her voice drifts off. Something like sadness coating her words.

The urge to hold her has me on my feet in seconds, my arms circling her from behind. She doesn't wait to turn to face me, hers looping around my middle. The curve of her body into my front, automatic. A natural response for two people who have held each other every day for years.

Those amber eyes find mine again, searching. For what I don't know. I wish she'd say something. Anything.

My palm slides up over her cheek, my thumb caressing the apple. Leighton melts into my touch, her eyelids fluttering shut for a few brief moments before our eyes lock again.

Crackling electricity sparks between us. The kind you can't ignore and is nearly impossible to find. So intense I swear our bodies vibrate in unison.

"Fuck it," I whisper, before dropping my mouth to hers.

A small noise escapes her, but she only holds me closer, her hands fisting my shirt along my spine. Our mouths move together as if we've always known each other. As if our lips were meant to touch.

Everything about her is intoxicating. Her soft body in my hands. The swell of her chest pressing into mine. Her taste. Her smell. That tiny noise she keeps making as our mouths move.

We stumble, her back slamming into the bookcases, my palm crashing into it, keeping us upright.

Her fingers trail over my beard, looping around my neck. Our kiss only deepens. The both of us finding what we need in the other before the slam of her front door has her pulling away.

"Lee?" a male voice calls out.

"Yeah. In here, Mike." She slips out from under my arm, brushing her hair down so it lies flat again. Her ragged breaths barely slowing before a man appears in the doorway.

I want to know who the fuck this guy is that just let himself into her house. I'm searching my memories, trying to remember what her best friend's husband's name is, but I'm drawing a blank. Regardless I don't like that he just barged in here.

"You were supposed to— Oh!" he stops short, carrying the basket I'd left Leighton this afternoon.

"Shoot. I knew I forgot something at your house earlier." She grabs the basket from him, walking it into the kitchen before joining us back in the family room. "Mike, this is Gavin. Gavin, Mike."

Her voice seems even, but there's something in her eyes that makes me think otherwise. One thumb driving into her opposite palm as she waits for us to shake.

Mike stretches his hand toward mine. "Nice to meet you." Then he turns back to Leighton. "You were supposed to call me if you needed a ride."

She pats his cheek with a wide grin. "I didn't. Now go home. Tell Allie I'm having fun and haven't been murdered."

Mike grumbles something under his breath that sounds a lot like, "There go my balls." His retreat is as swift as his entry. The click of a lock indicating he secured the door as he exited. The possessive man in me writhing knowing another guy has a key.

"How many people have keys to your house?" I question, stalking toward her before wrapping my arms around her waist.

I'm hoping she wants to pick up where we left off because I can't wait to taste her again.

"Just them. No one else to bother me tonight."

Her smile flashes once more before she pulls my head down to hers and kisses me stupid.

Damn. I'm already a goner.

Chapter 11

LEIGHTON

I HADN'T EXPECTED GAVIN to still be here at two in the morning.

We ate, which included me force-feeding him wings and fries when his salad came with wilted leaves and shriveled vegetables that looked a week old. He took it like a champ, but if we're going to keep hanging out, he's going to need to loosen the reins on the rabbit food.

Then we just talked, mostly about random stories from college and his time on the football team. That explained why his last name sounded familiar. He wasn't one of our star players, but he'd had enough field time to blow out his knee. After that, he quit and focused on his academics, but he stayed close to his former teammates.

Placing a hand on his knee, his eyes meet mine. "I'm sure you're tired, but I feel bad letting you drive home so late."

"I am tired, but it was worth it to spend more time with you."

My cheeks heat in response to his words. Delicate butterflies beating their wings in my belly, far too excited by his answer.

I shouldn't do it, but since I'm suddenly living on the edge, I figure Allie will be proud of where my thoughts are straying.

"Why don't you just stay? I haven't set up the guest room yet, but I have a king-sized bed."

He looks like he's about to choke to death, and suddenly, I want to take my words back.

Shit, that sounded so forward.

No doubt, several unwanted expectations were thrown out there unintentionally.

"But, um, you don't have to. I'm not trying to have sex with you. I just meant I have a big bed, so you'll have no problem fitting and—"

His audible groan stops my word vomit. The pained expression on his face making me want to shrivel up and die. This is so fucking embarrassing. I've always been awkward when I start dating someone—really with any new person I meet for a while. I guess that doesn't improve with time or age.

Jumping up from the couch, I bolt down the hall and up the stairs.

I can't stand seeing his face look like he's in physical pain. The hope of something new blossoming between us withering away, thinking about his pinched features. Digging the heels of my hands into my eyes does nothing to erase the images.

Stupid. Stupid. Stupid.

Tossing myself face-first onto the bed, I snatch a pillow screaming into it for a few brief moments. Then I force myself into silence, listening for the opening of the front door or the rumble of his SUV pulling down my drive.

I'm not sure how long has passed while I listen, only for the bed to dip next to me.

"This is a big bed, but if you sleep like that, my legs will definitely be dangling off the edge all night."

Peering up at him, humor dances in his eyes. "Gavin, I—"

He presses a finger to my lips. "For the record, I wasn't expecting sex. I'm lucky I got to kiss you in the first place, and I hope you'll let me again. Second, thank you for letting me stay." He lowers his finger, only to bring his thumb to the bottom lip I was about to bite down on. "Are you going to let me kiss you again?"

I can only nod before his lips softly press to mine, my chin held between his long fingers. His grip is firm, keeping me right where he wants me. Right where I desire to be.

It only takes seconds for heat to explode through my body. His long frame lowering atop mine, only to nestle between my legs as I settle on my back. He's hard as a rock as his pelvis flexes forward. My core drenched and wanting more.

"Gavin," I breathe as his lips trail over my jaw.

"Just another minute." The heat from his lips scorch my skin, my palms finding their way to his bare back beneath the hem of his shirt. "Sweetheart, I like your hands on me."

"I like it too." My hips roll up into his, his groan loud as he drops his face to my neck.

"I'm going to stop now."

"You—" The protest dies on my tongue.

I don't want him to stop. My body hungrily craves him. It's ravenous for his touch and his attention.

I meant what I said. I'm not the type to just sleep around. Hell, I've only been with two men my whole life. But as his hard length rocks against me, I'm willing to take back those words.

"No." His eyes find mine. "I am going to stop because I already know I have to have you, but I want to do it right."

The muscles between my legs pulse as if he had just given the most heartfelt proposal of all time. Their chants of "Take me now!" growing harder to ignore the longer his weight presses into me. More insistent, the longer I grind against the roll of his hips into my eager core.

Accepting his boundaries, I search for a practical topic change. A way to keep this from getting awkward—my specialty.

"I don't have anything for you to sleep in." He only chuckles, rolling off me before pulling me to my feet. "And um, I should maybe tell you I don't sleep with pants, so we can build like a pillow barrier or whatever if you want."

He pulls me to him, softly kissing my jaw, my cheek, and then my mouth. "I sleep in my underwear. You can sleep in whatever you like to wear, but I'm a cuddler. I doubt a few pillows will keep me from finding you in the night."

Well, shit.

This is going to be a long night.

My shirt clings to my back, the heat of another body reminding me that just a few hours ago Gavin climbed into bed with me.

It took every ounce of control not to stare at his crotch. His erection stood proud beneath his boxer briefs. The man didn't even try to hide it as he pulled me into his chest, kissing me tenderly before ordering me to sleep. Feeling dismissed, I'd rolled over to my side, putting my back to him, and forced my eyes shut.

Thank the heavens for big dicks, but maybe what I thought was large was average. My final thoughts before I eventually drifted off.

Gavin's body is perfection. His sculpted frame landing somewhere between lean muscle and low-end bulk. More hair than I'm typically into lines his chest and upper torso. None of it manscaped like so many men choose to do these days. That's just weird.

His beard tickles my cheek as he snuggles in closer. The shocks of gray throughout only adding to his appeal.

Gavin warned me he was a cuddler, but we'd fallen asleep on opposite edges of the bed. As if we were magnets drawn together in our sleep, we're both in the center of the mattress now. His heavy leg drapes over mine, pinning me against him with his front pressed against my back.

I wiggle a little, testing the strength of his hold. I have a tendency to wake up in the middle of the night to pee. Every reminder to ease up on the endless bottles of water before bed failing to keep me from doing just that. Old habits really do die hard.

"Mmm, Lee, stop moving," he groans. I immediately freeze. The feel of him swelling to attention behind me and using my nickname has me nearly turning feral.

It's been far too long since I've been laid... obviously.

"Um, I need to pee."

He groans again, releasing me and flopping to his back. His abs flex as he shifts, but he keeps his eyes closed.

"Hurry back. I'm cold," he practically whines.

Shuffling out of the room, I head for the bathroom down the hall. No way I am going to let that sexy man listen to me pee.

Gavin is still stretched out where I left him when I reenter my room, easing the door shut behind me so I don't wake him again. Moving as little as possible while climbing back into bed, a yelp slips free as his heavy arm wraps around me. His lips find my jaw, then my mouth, as I turn my head.

"Did you brush your teeth?" he questions, his eyes popping open. That blue is still bright even in the dark. A bottomless Antarctic sea just waiting for me to get lost in their depths.

"Uh..."

"You're too cute." He kisses me again, his tongue sweeping across the seam of my mouth. I open up for him, my hands slipping into his short hair.

He devours my mouth like a starving man. Our tongues warring, his long frame slipping on top of mine. The grind of our hips against one another making me want to take back what I said. If he asked to have sex right now, I would. My body wants it, and so do I.

Just as quickly as I had the thought, he breaks the kiss, dropping his forehead to mine.

"What's wrong?" I pant.

His head shakes, but he doesn't lift it. "Sweetheart, nothing." His palm finds my cheek, that thumb stroking as he looks into my eyes. "Nothing is wrong. I'm just having the damnedest time controlling myself with you."

Running my fingers down his spine, his body shudders under my touch. The muscles rolling in waves in response to my feather-light brush over his heated skin.

My words barely come out above a whisper. "You don't have to."

He brushes a strand of hair back off my face, placing a quick kiss on my lips. "Yes, I do. You told me you weren't having sex with me. I don't think that was just you trying to make sure I didn't expect it. You're a good woman and I try to be a good man, so I want to wait."

"Okay."

"Okay," he agrees. "Now, if you're good with it, I want to go back to cuddling you. Best sleep I've had in a long time."

"Okay."

Nuzzling into his side, I let my eyes fall shut. The stroke of his fingers along my arm lulling me to sleep faster than should be possible.

The last conscious thought is how lucky I am to have found a good one this time.

Hopefully.

Maybe.

Chapter 12

GAVIN

I can't remember the last time I wasn't up for my morning run. It's probably been years.

That's how well I slept, curled up around Lee. It was like she was made for me. Our bodies a perfect fit. Her presence exactly what I needed to slip out of the torturous mental gymnastics that taunt me, only shoved away by miles of pavement beneath my feet.

It had taken every bit of strength to get out of that bed with her this morning. Even more to walk out the door, promising I would call her later this afternoon. At least this time, through all of our conversation, I hadn't forgotten to get her number.

When she kissed me goodbye this morning, it felt so natural. Like two people who have known each other forever. Like I was just heading off to work, and she'd be there waiting for me at home later.

I fell hard and fast for Jen like this, too. The reminders of how that ended filtering to the forefront of my mind as I enter my apartment.

Jen and I were hot and heavy from the moment we met. We slept together that first night and never stopped. Then there were more nights spent together than apart, so when we graduated, it was a no-brainer to move in together. We were still so blissfully happy. So mindlessly in love.

But life was something we were never prepared for—not the reality of it. I wish I could say there was a good reason Jen and I drifted apart, but there wasn't. We both worked long hours. We both had our own friend groups. And the older we got, the more bridal showers, bachelor and bachelorette parties, weddings, and baby showers we attended. All our friends and relatives were moving forward in life. Yet, we weren't.

We were still just those kids who met junior year. We still loved each other, but we could both feel our love slowly fading with time. Eventually, nothing was left except a friendship, if you could even call it that. We became roommates who passed each other in the hall. Then, there was nothing at all but fond memories.

Ember thinks I'm heartbroken over Jen, but really, it's the loss of having someone to love as much as I once loved her. It meant everything to be someone's partner. I watched it my whole life with our parents, grandparents, and aunts and uncles. Every last one of them has an amazing marriage. Why wouldn't I want that for myself?

"Where have you been?" Ember's voice sounds from behind me.

My feet leap two inches in the air before I crash into the wall. *Fuck*, she is always doing this. Only this time, I'd been so distracted I wasn't prepared.

"I was out. Why are you in my apartment? Again?"

"It was closer than going home last night. We had a few too many at the bar."

My eyes press shut with gratitude. It was something I always told Ember while she attended school out here. If she ever didn't feel safe or had too much to drink and needed to come here, she always could. She took that to mean any time she wanted, including when she needed quiet to study.

"You didn't throw up in my bathroom again, did you?"

She scoffs, shuffling down the hall to hug me around the middle. "Mmm, I love you. And no. No vomit to clean up this time."

"Love you too." I hold her back. Many don't understand how we're so close, but I think it's because we're so far apart in age. At twelve, I was old enough to do things for her and help take care of her. Before I left for school, I was her taxi, her babysitter, and, oftentimes, her chaperone. It's an interesting relationship getting to be a best friend and a sibling. One I would never trade.

"Now, where were *you* last night? I was tracking your location, but didn't recognize the address."

"You're such a creep."

"I learned from the best," she grins, throwing herself onto my sectional couch.

"I was on a date." I avert my eyes so maybe she won't see how giddy I am. Now is not the time for her endless questions.

Her mouth drops open. "An all-night date? Ohmigod, please tell me you finally got some."

I groan loudly, covering my face with my arm as I sink into the cushions. "Can we not?"

"Okay, fine. Where did you meet her?"

"Your Valentine's Day party, actually."

Her nose scrunches, pointer tapping her soft chin. "Really? That explains why you just up and disappeared. Do I get to meet her soon? Are you taking her on the cabin trip?"

Ember's deep brown eyes are wide as she waits for me to answer her barrage of questions. I'd thought about asking Lee if she would come with me next weekend, but then chickened out, not wanting to scare her off.

"We're new. I don't think she's going to want to go to the middle of nowhere, West Virginia, with me and my friends."

"Holy shit!" Ember suddenly pops up from her sprawled position. "Is this the woman you were trying to cryptically ask me about?"

Yet another groan breaks free, my head tipping back with a grunted, "Yes."

Ember only cackles, stretching back out on the couch. She's tall for a woman, with the same lean frame as me. She hates it. All the hot guys aren't tall—according to her—and she wishes she had curves to fill out her clothes the way her friends do. Unfortunately, genetics had other plans.

"You should ask her. It can't hurt." My sister suddenly bolts upright, turning to face me. How she can stand this much movement with a hangover is insane. "But if she says yes, keep her away from Craig. He might be hot as hell, but you know him."

My eyes press shut again. Nothing has ever happened between my sister and my best friend, but she loves to remind me how good-looking she thinks he is. Fortunately, I've never seen her date a blond, so I think we're safe there. "Okay, I'll ask her."

Leaning back in my seat again, I stare at nothing. I should be getting logged in for work, but there's no focus. There's only the press of Lee's body against mine through the night.

"Um, I meant now," Ember's face appears above mine.

"You're annoying, you know that?"

"Nah, you love me."

A small smile tugs at the corner of my mouth. "Yeah, I do."

"Okay, now, pronto. Love will not wait!" She snaps her fingers, strikes a pose, and then bursts into laughter.

Pulling my phone out of my pocket, I dial Lee's number.

It rings twice before she answers, clearly out of breath. What is she doing?

"Hey, um, can you talk for a minute?"

"Yeah. Yeah, of course," she breathes. "Bye, honey," she calls to someone. "Sorry, I was dropping my niece at school."

Rubbing a hand over my bearded cheek, my stomach is in knots. "Oh, right? I hope I didn't make you late this morning."

"No, not at all. Allie got a flat tire and asked me to come save the day while she was waiting for roadside. I'm on my way back to her now."

"I hope she's okay."

She snickers, "It's Allie. She'll be fine. I'm more worried about the roadside person they send her. They better have thick skin."

I can't help the tiny chuckle that escapes me before my nerves shove me back into the moment. "So, I'm calling because, uh, do you remember that cabin trip I mentioned?"

"Yeah, sounds like a lot of fun." Her turn signal chirps in the background. The *tick, tick, tick* somehow cranking my sweat glands into overdrive.

"Well, I was wondering if you might want to come. With me, that is?" The line is silent. Only that airy sound the Bluetooth makes when you're driving filling my ears. "There should be enough beds you don't need to share with me. Unless you want to, because we already did. Shit!"

Her giggle comes through the line, causing my dick to animatedly twitch. Angling my body away from my sister in case it wants to stand at attention, I press the phone harder against my ear.

"If you really want me to come, I should be able to." The smile in her response draws out mine. It was there in the soft lilt of her words, even though I'm not there to witness it.

A silent breath releases from me. One that had been trapped in my lungs, making them burn intensely, hoping her answer would be just that. "Yeah, I would."

"Okay. Let me just make sure Allie didn't need me for anything. I'll text you in a little bit, okay?"

"Sounds good. Drive safe, sweetheart."

Then she ends the call.

Ember snickers behind me.

"What?" I snap. My tone clipped but with almost no bite to it.

Ember shifts to her knees, grinning like a fool from her side of the couch. "Big brother, you have it so bad. Can I come too so I can watch this trainwreck unfold?" Her body tilts side to side in anticipation of me finally allowing her to come on one of our friend trips. Something I've never allowed for a multitude of reasons.

"Fuck you, Em. Go home."

"Nah, I'm still hungover. I'm going to nap until class."

Ruffling her hair, I sprint off to my room. I need a few minutes alone.

A few moments of quiet to process my good fortune. Luck I've been waiting for over the past five years. I can't believe she said yes.

Inhaling a deep breath, I sit on the edge of the bed.

This is either going to be great or the trainwreck Ember called.

At least I have over a week to spend more time with that woman before we find out. Maybe then we can edge closer to great.

Chapter 13

LEIGHTON

Fortunately, it didn't take roadside long to get to Allie.

They were nearly done changing her tire by the time I arrived. Her arms crossed over her chest, and her hip cocked to the side as she waited with a skeptical eye.

She'd sped off to work after that, leaving me to my own devices.

I decided it was as good a time as any to unpack some of the remaining boxes shoved into one of the guest rooms. Maybe even order some furniture so the girls have somewhere to sleep when they stay over. The last time the three of us piled into my bed, and though they're small, I still ended up with feet, knees, and hands in my face, ribs, and back.

Still, I wouldn't change it. At this rate, they may be the only kids I ever get.

It's been amazing spending so much time with my nieces. Allie, Mike, and those girls are the only family I have to speak of. I have a few great aunts and uncles, but we were never close. Truthfully, I'm not sure I know their names or could even pick them out in a lineup.

No, when Mom and Dad passed, it truly was just me on my own.

Dragging a box from the corner, I search for where I wrote the contents on it. The fact that I didn't basically confirms it's likely a hodgepodge of random things I never got rid of. I am the type who keeps everything—a hoarder in my own right.

It could be the most meaningless item, and I will find a way to get attached to it. My brain constructs reasons why I can't get rid of it. This is also why I have an obscene amount of clothing I never wear. Seventy percent of the items likely still have the tags because they either didn't fit at the time or were something I saw someone else wear and thought I would, too. That's a big fat nope.

Before my parents left, I worked a lot, but I had some semblance of a social life, too. Sure, it was mostly my colleagues, but if it's decent company, it doesn't matter if that's who you're spending your nights with at the bar.

Cutting through the tape and flipping open the flaps, I wish I hadn't. A million flaming hot knives drive into my chest and gut. My knees wobble as a sob breaks free. The choked sound alarming in my ears.

I wish I had labeled the damn box.

My ass crashes to the floor, the carpet barely cushioning my fall as my hand cups over my mouth and the sobs tear through my body. I hadn't kept much from my parent's house. Honestly, I didn't have the room for it, and I didn't want to sit there and cry every two seconds, tormented by pieces of them sprinkled throughout my renal house.

This lone box contains everything I kept of them: Dad's favorite baseball hat, Mom's pearls, their wedding photo, and the random portrait I drew of our family in elementary school—things that would mean nothing to anyone else but me.

Tears burn behind my eyes before I let them fall. Fat, angry droplets soaking into my threadbare t-shirt. Every bit of anguish I've kept locked inside for months rushes free. An exorcism of all the things I tried to bury deep so I could carry on.

Life isn't fair. They were too young to die. I wasn't ready.

The corner of the blanket Mom attempted to crochet pokes up. My fingers curl over the lumpy pastel mess before pulling it free. She picked up the hobby when I started PA school, a way to occupy her time because I wasn't around as much then.

I clutch it to my chest, inhaling the scent. The fibers still smell like her expensive perfume. It was supposed to be a blanket, but it resembles an amoeba more. She kept up the hobby but never became proficient at it.

"I miss you, Mom," I whisper to no one.

Then I bury my face in the woven threads and cry. I cry until my throat and lungs burn. Until every tear dries. Until I can't breathe and then I can, just sitting there in a trance, staring at nothing. Thinking about nothing. Feeling nothing.

It's hours of me sitting curled up with the blanket before I notice my phone ringing downstairs.

Angrily wiping my eyes, only to realize they must have dried long ago, I bolt to the kitchen.

"Hello!" My breaths are heavy, elbows leaning on the island. Those same knives resuming their twisting routine as if never interrupted.

"You okay?" Allie questions.

"Yeah. I was unpacking. What's up?" My voice is an octave too high. Too uneven. But Allie doesn't push for once. A small mercy.

"I need a favor."

It's odd that Allie would call me in the middle of the afternoon asking for anything. Or maybe it's just that since I moved in next door, I've gotten so used to her barging into my house that I forgot we communicated in any other way besides face-to-face.

"What's up?"

"Can you pick up the girls? Mike's mother broke her arm, and his father called, begging us to come out tonight. I don't want to take the girls since we'll be gone for a few days."

"Yeah, of course. I hope she's okay." A perfect distraction from the crippling grief fighting to pull me under its violent waves.

I can practically hear Allie's eye roll. "I'm sure the old bat is fine. Mike is going to pack their bags, and we already have a babysitter for tomorrow night since you'll be working."

"Um, okay. Would it be easier on them if I stayed at your place?"

"They like your house better," she chuffs. "Okay, gotta run. Thank you. Love you!"

"Love you, too. Bye," I chuckle.

Heading back upstairs, I enter the same room I'd been in, staring at that open box. Shoving the blanket back inside, I fold the flaps closed, frustrated I don't have tape to seal it completely. There's no part of me ready to interact with the contents. Not now. Maybe never.

I can only hope that one day I'll be ready to open that box, but it certainly isn't today.

My heart isn't ready to do it alone. Not yet.

Grabbing my coat, keys, and wallet, I know I need to get out of the house. The fridge is practically empty, and if I'm going to have the kids for a few days, I need to grab the things they like.

I check my phone just before I pull out of my driveway, noticing that red circle of doom indicating a notification on my texting app.

Opening it up, a huge grin takes over my face. Erasure of how I just spent the last few hours drowning in my grief beginning.

Gavin: Thank you for agreeing to come to the cabin.

Gavin: I promise we'll have fun.

I sit there in silence while my car hums around me for a few minutes. Words string together in my head. None of them are good enough to be a cute and flirtatious response.

Me: There is that whole trend about skipping dating and going straight to baecation

The moment I hit send, I immediately want to take it back. There were too many assumptions in that statement. But the dots dance along the bottom of the screen almost immediately.

Gavin: Baecation?

Gavin: Kind of catchy

Gavin: I think I'll adopt it.

A snort leaves me before I drop my phone into my cupholder, pulling out of my driveway.

There shouldn't be this much traffic at one in the afternoon on a random Thursday. But I guess I shouldn't be surprised when I walk into the grocery store, and it's full of Stepford Wives and soccer moms in their perfectly curated outfits and athleisure wear, pushing carts full of everything they could get their hands on.

To say I feel out of place would be an understatement as I grab my own empty shopping cart and head to the snack aisle first.

Stopping in front of the cookies, I pull several packages off the shelf. I may not have always been there as my girls grew up, but I know everything they like. I mailed them care packages and video-chatted with them while they opened them. Everything Allie keeps for them in her house, I do too.

"Your kids must love you," the woman next to me snickers.

"Excuse me." I don't mean to sound so indignant, but I didn't particularly care for her tone. Not to mention how does she know I wasn't planning to have a fat party all alone on my couch? Why is there this assumption that after a certain age, you likely have kids if you're buying snacks?

"All the sugar. I limit it for mine, and they hate me for it." Her tone suddenly changes, shoulders rolling forward in defeat as she snatches reduced fat Cheez-Its from the shelf.

"Perks of being the cool aunt," I shrug.

She only gives me a sad smile before moving down the rest of the aisle.

Such a weird interaction.

But one is all I need, so I quickly make my way down each aisle, throwing more than I need in my cart before bolting from the store.

I'll be doing delivery from now on.

Chapter 14

GAVIN

It wasn't long after Ember went to sleep off her hangover in the guest room that I left for the office.

Sitting home attempting to work wasn't going to serve anyone well today.

I'm too busy freaking out over Leighton agreeing to go on this trip with me. Too preoccupied with memories of her from last night. That giggle and the way she laughed as we walked down memory lane together. The way her eyes sparkle when she is excited and the feel of her pliant body beneath my palms. But more than anything, it's the way she looks at me.

An expression I can't quite describe. A combination of awe and lust. Pining and fascination. Comfort and joy. The way that woman looks at me is like every amazing feeling in the world combined. And I'm terrified of losing it.

I'd picked at my breakfast wrap for twenty minutes, attempting to analyze how her voice sounded before I found myself texting her.

This was followed by an agonizing two hours of waiting for her response. I'm always like this when I meet someone new: eager to jump in when they might not be.

But I have never invited another woman on our quarterly trips besides Jen. She always joined us for the cabin trip and the exotic beaches in the summer but often skipped the other two, either because of work commitments or just because she needed her space, as she liked to put it. For Jen, reliving our younger years as adults every year like clockwork was ridiculous.

"Honestly, traveling with the seven of you gets old," she'd once scoffed. *"You all still act like the college boys you were."*

She's not wrong. That young streak has never really left us when we're together. As if time has frozen our joint personalities while we still physically aged. Normally, I don't worry about our raucous behavior. We are who we are. The spouses and girlfriends have been around long enough to ignore us at this point, so why pretend to be any different?

But now I'm nervous. I want Leighton to like them as much as I want them to like her.

No, it goes beyond that. Need is a more appropriate word because I already know Leighton has taken hold of my heart. A capture so perfect it could never be repeated.

It's been a sluggish work day, my eyes not believing it's only four when I finally finish the analysis I'd been working on. One of the few accounts since I started working for my company that literally drives my blood pressure through the roof. Sky is not the limit this time.

The client takes massive risks—too many. His portfolio is impressive, sure, but many of his successes have been pure luck. In the end, he makes our job difficult by doing as he pleases.

Rubbing my thumbs against my eye sockets, a heavy yawn leaves me.

The vibration of my phone against my desk suddenly forcing my back ramrod straight. Several pens and a stapler crash to the floor as my hands launch forward, snatching it. A tremble works its way through my body, tapping the notification.

Leighton: Sorry! Had to do a grocery run. Why are there so many people there in the middle of the day?

Me: I wish I could tell you.

Me: Are you back home now? Please don't tell me you text and drive.

Leighton: Yes. I'm home.

Leighton: About to pop in a movie and order pizza.

Me: My kind of night…

Leighton: Mine too *grinning emoji*

I can only stare at my phone, waiting for the dots to dance again, but they don't. Was that an invitation?

My heart hammers, sitting stock still staring at the screen, waiting for another text or a call. Some divine sign that she told me what she was doing because she wants to spend more time with me. Deciding it was, I shut down my computer and head home to change.

Impromptu date night sounds great.

Every light shines brightly inside Leighton's house when I pull into her driveway.

Grabbing the bouquet, and the massive bag of snacks and wine I stopped at the store for, I make my way to her front door.

It takes several deep breaths to calm me before I ring the bell. The sounds of bare feet clapping against the wood before I hear her shout, "Don't open that!" making me take a step back.

Seconds later, she yanks open the door.

Fuck, she's gorgeous.

Her hair is a mess. Eyes wide as they rake down my frame before meeting my gaze again. Her sweatpants hug her thighs just the right amount, and her shirt hangs off her shoulder, exposing smooth skin.

Then two little blonde girls come up behind her, the smaller one clinging to her leg.

"Hi," I quirk a crooked grin, suddenly embarrassed. I should have called or asked if she was alone. Hell, she could have had another man here, or I don't know.

"What are you doing here?" she sounds breathless, smoothing the little girl's hair.

"I, uh. Well, you said... I guess I thought..."

Sweat beads on my forehead. Leighton chokes me up as if I'm nothing more than a teenage boy.

"Sorry." She shakes her head. "Come in. Let me take that." She reaches for the bag, but I pull it out of reach.

"You can take these." She tentatively takes the flowers from me, her brow scrunching as if unsure of what she's holding. But she brings them to her face, inhaling long and deep before lowering the colorful array once more.

"Girls, go back in the family room and finish your pizza."

They immediately take off running, barely around the corner, before she throws her arms around my neck, hugging me close. Trying not to smack her with the bag, I hold her back.

Just as quickly, she lets me go. "Thank you. They're beautiful. Did you eat? Do you need a drink or pizza?"

A chuckle leaves me, her lips clamping shut. "Pizza sounds good."

She leads us to the kitchen and grabs me a plate. "Okay, we have cheese, Hawaiian, pepperoni, and veggie." The scrunch of her nose accompanying the last choice she lists.

"Why do you have so much? Is someone else here?" My voice rises a little higher than I want. Her eyes meeting mine before her head cocks to the side has me second-guessing my decision to come here for the hundredth time in so many minutes.

"No. Just me and the girls. We all eat different types and always get a wild card pizza with a different topping."

"Which was the wild card?"

"Veggie." She wrinkles her nose, opening the box, the entire pizza still intact. "I'm guessing this will be your pick health nut."

Dropping the bag on the counter, I pull three slices out and put them on the plate.

"You guessed right."

My eyes drift down to her lips. I'd hoped to kiss her the moment I walked through the door, but then I saw those little girls.

"Feel free to eat in here or in the family room with the girls," she says before starting out of the kitchen.

"Wait, where are you going?"

"Upstairs. They'll be here for a few days, so I bought a bed, and I'm trying to put it together."

Another one of our staring contests ensues. Neither of us budging until the older of the two girls waltzes into the kitchen, grabbing another slice of Hawaiian pizza. "Auntie Lee, who is that?"

"This is my friend, Gavin. Gavin, this is one of my nieces, Abby, and the smaller one is Tori."

"Nice to meet you." I reach out a hand to shake hers. She does quickly before skipping off with her plate. "Did you eat?" My molars grind already expecting the answer will be no.

"I will after—"

"Go grab yourself some pizza. I'll eat really quick and then go put the bed together."

"Gavin, you don't have to do that." Her eyes cast down to her bare feet. Her toes wiggling against the hardwood floors as if looking for purchase.

Stepping into her space, I put the plate on the island, staring down at her. My hand finds her waist, pulling her closer, just out of view of the opening between the family room and the kitchen. Then I press my mouth to hers. Soft and all too brief. "I want to. Please go eat."

She drops two slices of pepperoni pizza on her plate before leading me into the family room. Her nieces are sprawled on the floor, their eyes glued to the massive wall-mounted TV I somehow missed last night. I have no idea what movie this is, but they're so into it that they don't even notice us joining them.

Colorful blobs or creatures fill the screen, their song piercing through the silence of us eating. I have no idea what this movie is, but somehow, it's entertaining.

It only takes me five minutes to scarf down the pizza before I wander upstairs.

More pictures line the stairwell. I assume the people captured repeatedly are her parents. I pause at one at the top of the steps, with what could only be her as a little girl. Her front teeth are missing, and her eyes are pressed shut as she laughs wildly, held up in the air by the man who must be her father. Their features are a match.

I know they passed relatively close together. She'd told me that much. Yet, they are another wish on my endless list when it comes to that woman downstairs. I'll never meet them, but maybe in another life, I'll get the chance.

Wandering down the hall, the first door I come to yields what I'm looking for. There are pieces of the frame everywhere. Screws lie in piles on the single dresser adorning the far wall. The mattress still rolled up in its box by the window.

"What the hell?" I mumble to no one.

"I know." Her voice at my back startles me, an involuntary jump leaving me clutching my chest and breathing hard. "I've never been gifted at building things on my own, but I've always figured it out." Her hand finds my mid-back. "I didn't mean to scare you. Just wanted to make sure you found the room."

"You're fine." I pull at her wrist so she shifts to stand in front of me. Her eyes search mine again before I bend to kiss her. This one less reserved than the brief touch I'd given her downstairs. Our mouths slanting and her hips rolling into me as I back her into the doorframe. The moment my mouth catches her moan, she pulls away, her teeth sinking into her bottom lip. "Go downstairs." I give her hip a slight squeeze. "I'll be down when I'm done."

She only smiles softly. "Thank you, Gavin."

Chapter 15

LEIGHTON

THERE ARE TWO THINGS I've learned about myself today.

First, I could never be a single mother. This morning, getting the kids fed and ready for school without forgetting anything nearly brought me to tears.

Allie has been doing it for years. Sure, she has Mike, but he's usually gone before the girls even shuffle downstairs for breakfast. That's the way of Corporate America, I guess.

Tori didn't want to brush her teeth at the same time as Abby. Abby couldn't remember where she left her math homework, so she zoomed around the house searching for it. She found it in her backpack, where she had put it. Tori wanted to sing one more song before we left, so Abby told her to stop being such a baby, which resulted in actual tears.

I left both their lunch boxes on the kitchen counter and had to turn around after we'd already gotten ten minutes away. Somehow, I got them to school on time, but man was that a circus.

The second thing I learned about myself is I am not built for the night shift anymore. It's been years since I had to do one. Perks of staying employed at the same hospital for eight years. I'd earned the privilege of only working the day shift unless someone needed coverage.

Though I'm a night owl, working a twelve-hour third shift is a different beast. One that sucks the life right out of you. The atmosphere transforms, and the patients turn into gremlins—in my mind.

I'd hesitated to apply to my alma mater's medical center. It seemed so bittersweet knowing this was the one medical school I wanted to attend, intern, and then work for so long. It was the dream. OSU's Wexner Medical Center was the whole reason I decided to come here. One that shriveled up and died before I could blink.

But part of me felt like I could finally let go of that disappointment if I just worked here. Those old wounds could heal, and I could leave behind a future that obviously wasn't meant for me.

In truth, I had expected it to be filled with nothing but college kids at night. However, this medical center prides itself on being the best of the best. Add in that it's only one of two level-one trauma centers in central Ohio, and we're busy as hell all the time.

"How are you holding up?" a nurse slides up beside me as I review the current chart.

"I think I'm too old for nights."

She laughs loudly, shaking her head. "But that's when all the best stuff happens." She winks, and then she disappears into a room a few feet from us.

And she wasn't wrong.

The night is a blur between visiting with patients and texting the sitter. The girl probably hates me right now, but there's no way I'm not going to keep checking on my girls.

My anxiety is taking on a life of its own, swirling through me in a vortex that only gains speed with each passing minute of my separation from my girls. Leaving my nieces alone overnight, even though Allie told me I have nothing to worry about, is yet another new leap of faith I'm having to grapple with. They're with the same young woman who has been watching the girls since they were babies. Just the same, a protective nature lives within me. I don't know this woman, so my trust doesn't necessarily align with Allie and Mike's.

Knowing she has been around for ten years does nothing to calm my firing nerves and twisting intestines.

Every moment I am not visiting with a patient is spent worrying about those babies. They should be fast asleep, but a heavy boulder sits at the base of my belly, wondering if they're not. They've stayed at my house countless times, but never without me.

I only relax when I pull into my driveway at 7:22 a.m., heading straight upstairs to the bedroom, where they are both still sound asleep in the bed Gavin built.

Their soft snores make them appear so innocent. The even pace settling my racing heart as I lean against the doorframe. I only watch them for a few more minutes before slipping into my own room, desperate for a shower.

Pulling my phone out of my jacket pocket, I check my notifications again. A habit that's become more prominent since I met Gavin.

Gavin: I hope you had a good night at work and a good morning gorgeous.

Gavin: I loved your nieces, by the way.

A smile tugs at my cheeks.

Me: They loved you too

Me: Tori was quite upset you were gone when she woke up in the morning. She wanted to finish the puzzle you two started.

Gavin: Tell her I can come over anytime...

My cheeks ache from smiling so widely. It seems too perfect that I already like this guy so much, and my nieces do, too. It's so rare that I warm up to someone so effortlessly.

Me: I'll tell her.

Gavin: Get some sleep sweetheart. I'll call you this afternoon.

Tossing my phone on the bed, I'm quick to jump in the shower, knowing I'm not getting more than an hour of sleep before my two gremlins wake up. Thank goodness they take after me and their mother—we are not morning people.

Scalding water washes over me. It's my ritual after a shift. A need to wash off all the filth of the night. I feel like I'm raw after, but I can't sleep unless I do.

Within twenty minutes, I'm showered, lotioned, and climbing under the covers, but my mind won't shut down. Thoughts of Gavin keep swirling through my head. Ignoring my best judgment, I text him.

> **Me: Are you busy?**

It seems like hours before he texts back. In reality, it's likely no more than two minutes.

> **Gavin: Just leaving for the gym.**

> **Me: After your run?**

> **Gavin: Yup! I'm getting old. Gotta throw in a little weight training sometimes too.**

> **Me: Solid point.**

> **Me: Okay have fun.**

Those dreaded dots dance across the bottom of the screen several times before they disappear. With a huff, I flop to my back before my phone vibrates again. Once. Twice.

Looking at the screen, it's Gavin calling.

"Hello?"

"Are you okay?" His breaths are heavy as the sounds of shuffling clothing and zippers sound in the background.

"Yeah, why?"

"Well, you ask me what I'm doing, then just kind of brush me aside."

I go silent, my teeth sinking into my lip, wondering if I should tell him the real reason I texted.

The last thing any man wants is a clingy woman. Typically, I'm not, but something about Gavin makes me eager to have him around—all the time if our schedules allow for it.

"Lee."

Pressing my eyes shut for a few moments while cradling my phone to my chest, I let out a deep breath. Raising the phone back to my ear, my voice comes out shaky. "I, uh. I just wanted to see if you maybe wanted to come over."

The line goes silent for a few moments, more shuffling prominent in the background before the door closes.

"I'll be there in twenty."

Then he hangs up.

I can only lay there with a goofy grin on my face before I hear a car pull into the drive. My heart swelling knowing he dropped what he was doing to come here, and he doesn't even know why.

I race down the stairs to let him in, knowing the girls are still asleep.

"Hi," I breathe, opening the door. And instantly, that storm of grief that had been brewing inside me settles.

"Hey, sweetheart."

"Keep quiet. The girls are still asleep."

He slips off his shoes, dropping his hand in mine before we head upstairs. I close my door most of the way, leaving just a crack so the girls don't think they can't come in.

I don't waste any time climbing back under the warmth of my comforter, noticing Gavin is still standing by the door.

"Uh, Lee."

"What?"

He runs his hand over the back of his head, his muscles flexing under the long-sleeved shirt he's wearing. "I mean, I didn't stay the other night because we thought it would be better for the girls, so..."

The conversation had completely slipped my mind. It wasn't that I didn't want him to stay. I wanted to respect that I had someone else's children in my house, and this man is still kind of a stranger. Not to mention Allie hasn't met him.

Then, today, I just felt lonely, and I wanted someone to hold me. I wanted Gavin to hold me again. I needed his warmth to help my thoughts settle. Someone to remind me there's good in the world and safety within someone's arms.

Sighing loudly, he comes to sit on the edge of the bed. "What is it?"

"It's stupid."

Tilting my chin up with his fingers, his head dips. "I still want to hear whatever it is."

Covering my face with my hands, I groan loudly. "Sometimes... Sometimes I just need someone to hold me. I usually call Allie, but—"

I don't get the rest of the words out before he signals for me to scoot over, climbing in beside me. Where I stay tucked under the comforter, he stretches atop it, his arms looping around me in a protective hug.

Firm lips press to the top of my head. Once. Twice. And a third where he lingers just a few seconds longer than the first two.

"Go to sleep, Lee."

And I do, listening to the thrum of his heart.

Chapter 16

GAVIN

My suitcase lies open on the bed, each article of clothing neatly folded. For some reason, it seems like I've packed more than I normally do for this cabin weekend.

We dress more casually than not most of the time, enjoying outdoor activities and just lounging around the house. One dinner outfit is often all I've ever needed. Yet, glancing between my closet and my medium-sized suitcase, you'd think I'd packed everything I own.

Piles of shirts, jeans, and sweaters stare back at me. These are the clothes I wear when my henleys and sweatshirts aren't appropriate—attire that might impress Lee.

I have it so damn bad.

"Are you guys going for more than three days?" Ember questions sprawled out on my bed.

She showed up an hour ago and refused to leave. My baby sister has been here so frequently I'm starting to wonder if she's suddenly homeless.

Unlike Ember, I value alone time. I need it to gather my thoughts. In two days, I'll be taking my first... woman since Jen on a trip with me.

Not to mention I haven't seen Lee since she asked me to come over and hold her.

There was something so broken in the way she'd said it. As if she expected me to say no or didn't want to show the weakness of needing another person.

Lee is the type that gives the impression of wanting to do everything on her own. A tough side that makes me think she either doesn't like accepting help or doesn't know how. A trait I recognize because I've always been the giving type. Often to my own detriment.

Fortunately, my girl fell asleep almost instantly, her head on my chest, hand fisting my shirt. That day, Lee needed someone, and I am thankful I was the one she called.

It's a miracle I was able to unfold my body from hers when the girls came charging into her room an hour later.

I'd ushered them downstairs, cooking them breakfast and then completing the five thousand piece puzzle with Tori. Abby busied herself watching some TV show, but they seemed fine.

When Lee finally emerged downstairs, she looked just as gorgeous as always. Her hair was slightly mussed, and her cheeks a little rosy. Had her nieces not been there, I would have kissed her stupid, as fantasies of this becoming our reality morphed in my head.

She's been working almost non-stop since then, and the one day she had off, I was busy with a work event. Two ships passing in the night. A reminder of what my relationship with Jen had become.

A niggling feeling swirls through my stomach. A hunch telling me Lee and I won't become the same. Spending almost three days straight with her and then not seeing her at all has me on edge. Sure, we've texted every spare moment and talked on the phone every day, but it's not the same as spending time with a person. A person I crave, like the air I breathe.

"Earth to Gav," Ember's waving hand pulls me back to the present.

"Yeah! What?" I snap, distracted.

"What time do you pick up Craig?"

My eyes narrow on her. Not this shit again. The past week, Ember has brought up Craig more times than I care to count. Even though I trust them both, I am not taking chances putting them under the same roof with booze involved. "Don't worry about it."

"Knock it off. I'm just trying to make sure you're on time since you're clearly in Lala land thinking about your new girlfriend."

"She's not my girlfriend." The retort escapes as more of a whine than holding any real authority. In my mind, that's exactly what I would call Lee, but something tells me it's too soon to let that admission pass my lips. Not just to her but to anyone.

"Yeah, sure." Ember shrugs before hopping off the bed. "I have to get to class. Have a good trip."

She hugs me the way she always does before swiftly exiting my apartment.

My sister always could see right through me.

Why would I think today would be any different?

*   *   *

Reuniting with my best friend always feels like no time has passed. Maybe that's because we communicate constantly. Physically, we're apart every day, a fact Craig complains about at every turn. But he's the one who needed the big city and more opportunities.

Yet the distance has never dampened our relationship.

Maybe because when you meet someone that you connect with on a deeper level—friend or lover—you're always tethered to them. There's no separating you. That bond will only continue to strengthen with time. A reminder I gave myself when Jen and I officially called it quits. We weren't meant to be, and that's okay.

I'm suddenly shoved onto the edge of the couch, the motion nearly sending me hurdling to the floor with an embarrassing yelp.

"What the hell?" My tone is clipped, brow furrowed with agitation. Craig has an overly playful side sometimes. Most days, I can ignore it, but he'd interrupted my line of thought.

Thoughts that revolved around how good it felt to have Lee in my arms days ago and how for three days I hope to again. The crew can do as they please, but I'd be happy to stay cuddled in bed with her for those seventy-two hours.

There are no expectations of our relationship going any further than we have sexually. I'd be happy to kiss those soft lips for the rest of my life if she let me. But I'd be lying if I said I didn't want to let my hands roam all over her body. That I didn't want to feel what it's like to move inside her and hear whatever sounds she makes.

The bit of her I've touched wasn't enough. I want her bare skin and the curve of her ass filling my palms while my tongue wars with hers. My dick twitches just thinking about those thick thighs wrapped around my head while I taste her.

So yeah, I'm a bit pissed my buddy felt the need to interrupt the fantasy.

"I've been talking to you for like ten minutes. You didn't even hear a thing I said, did you?"

I hadn't. Truthfully, I don't even recall the croon of his southern accent in my ear.

"Sorry, no. I have a lot on my mind."

He only snorts, leaning back into the couch cushions. "Yeah, that chick."

My mouth presses into a straight line as my eyes narrow on him. Lee and I are new, but she's a lot more than just some chick. There's something special brewing between us, even if I might be the only one feeling it so far.

"It's just work stuff. I have a handful of big clients."

"Cut the shit, Gav! You always have high-profile clients," he rolls his eyes, chugging from his water bottle. "It's this woman that has you tied up in knots. You always get like this."

"Then why even ask the question?"

He only shrugs, tapping away at his phone as if the conversation no longer interests him, but I know Craig. He might be a playboy and act like he doesn't have a care in the world, but when it comes to his friends and his elder brother, he has the biggest heart. The guy wants every detail, every feeling, every thought.

"I like her a lot. Okay, that might be an understatement, but that doesn't matter." His snort gives me pause before I continue to spill my guts. "I'm nervous as hell about this weekend. I haven't seen her in three days."

He snorts again, dropping his phone to the couch between us. I swear, between him and Ember, if I didn't know better, I would think my two favorite people are pigs in disguise. "And that's fixable, yah know?"

"Yeah, it is, but not right now. We have dinner with Tyler and Ace in twenty." Jumping up from the couch, I snatch my coat from the front closet and my keys from the counter.

"Smooth." His laughter carries behind me.

We don't need twenty minutes to get to the restaurant that's only a five-minute walk away. I knew there was nothing "smooth" about me trying to get off the topic. But I can't hear the you're-getting-ahead-of-yourself speech right now, which is always followed by I-told-you-so.

Anxious butterflies fill my belly just thinking about giving him details on my girl. Like talking about me and Lee will jinx how awesome things are going so far. Something I can't have.

Sure, I've really enjoyed several of the women I've tried to date since Jen. They were smart, beautiful, funny, but they didn't burrow deep inside me, making me want to spend every fucking minute breathing the same air.

Jen was the last woman who made me feel this way, and honestly, we were kids then. Twenty-year-old children who hooked up one night and actually ended up liking each other before falling in love over the course of a few months. I've always been the type to have a girlfriend, but at the start of junior year, after I had to accept that I was no longer playing football, I had a rough few months of trying to find myself. It was then Jen and I met, and she was what I needed.

For years, she was that rock until we outgrew each other. Something we both agreed was no one's fault. Craig says I should have known it wasn't forever when I never had the desire to go out and buy the ring.

I'd never taken the time to look at things that way. When we were still in college, I used to tell her all the time that I was going to marry her after we graduated and got settled into our careers. Settled happened and then it gradually just kind of drifted away with our romantic love for each other.

There will always be a fondness in my heart for Jen. I am grateful for how she helped me love a different life than I planned back then, but there's not a single part of me that wants her back or what our life became.

"Let's go," I flag my best friend out the door.

His chuckle follows me. "This conversation isn't over because you're avoiding it."

But I don't respond. Resolute in my silence, I simply lead us to the elevators and then out of my building.

Craig and I walk in silence, something hovering between us. He has something to say. It's there on the tip of his tongue, but then Tyler runs up, lifting him in the air in a bear hug, and I'm off the hook.

For now, at least.

Chapter 17

LEIGHTON

Somehow, my schedule got switched to the night shift for the day. Normally, that wouldn't be an issue, except I agreed to go on a mountain getaway with Gavin and his friends.

Have I packed anything? *No.*

Do I need to go shopping? *Hell yes.*

Do I have time? *No.*

Not since I'm working tonight, and we leave at noon tomorrow. I'll literally have to bolt out of here, run home, shower, and then run out to the mall, come home, and shove it all in my suitcase. Truthfully, I pack by just throwing things in a bag in the first place but still. This is our first trip as a...

The word *couple* floats through my mind. A word that seems so natural. Is that what we are?

It's too soon. It has to be.

Or is it?

Gavin had called making me chicken piccata last night a date. My insides melting when he showed up with grocery bags in hand, ready to prove to me healthy, home-cooked food was superior to takeout.

Had Allie stayed, would it have still been a date or just the sexiest man alive cooking to prove a point? How quickly do people make things official these days?

She'd grilled him the way a best friend does and then promptly left before my nieces wandered over to find us. A wink thrown my way with a playful dare, *"Don't do anything I wouldn't do."*

The same words we've been slinging at each other since we met anytime we're about to get into a new adventure or have some fun.

I'd behaved, though. Sitting on one of my island barstools, I'd watched Gavin's every move. The way he marinated the chicken and tested the pasta cooking in a pot I forgot I had. Every undulation of his muscles as he'd stirred the lemon caper sauce with his back to me.

It's a miracle I was able to keep up with the conversation as I drooled over his body. Something he caught me doing several times when he'd turn around to grab an ingredient or ask where another kitchen item was.

A smile tugs at the corners of my mouth. My teeth digging into my bottom lip, hoping I get to see more of Gavin this weekend—preferably naked. As I pull up the next patient on my tablet, I fight to put it all out of my mind. There's nothing I can do about my lack of packing or imagination about Gavin's body while I'm here at work.

"Mr. Cochran, what brings you in today?" I ask, entering the next room.

The ED is a madhouse tonight. The types of patients are random, and there is no rhyme or reason to them—just jumbles of everything. The nurses and techs are swamped. It's not unusual for the PAs and even the doctors to go straight into the rooms on nights like this if there's a backlog of tests or patients getting worked up—anything to remain as efficient as possible.

But on nights like tonight, we'll fail at it anyhow.

"My stomach hurts," the mix of his gravely voice and whine grates on me. Grown men can be such babies.

It's insane.

They get a cold, and they're practically in tears.

Try surviving cramps every damn month and then complain. We won't even talk about pushing big-headed babies out of our vaginas.

"Alright, let's see here."

Pulling on gloves, I move to the side of his bed, fold down the sheet, and then lift his gown. Thank goodness this one kept his sweatpants on. Some are a bit too keen on taking everything off when it's not necessary, and I end up seeing a lot more than I bargained for.

He's not a small man, a little overweight, but his abdomen is clearly distended. His wince with each press of my fingertips, giving me a few ideas of what might be going on. "Any issues keeping food down?"

"No, but it hurts more after I eat." I only nod, continuing to palpate his abdomen and flanks.

"Okay, Mr. Cochran, just breathe normally. I am going to listen."

"Whatever you say, hun."

Listening in with my stethoscope practically confirms my suspicion. "Alright, Mr. Cochran, when was the last time you had a bowel movement?"

"I don't know. A few weeks, maybe."

It takes everything in me not to yell at the guy. "And have you been having stomach pain since then?" I palpate his flanks a little more, his twitching and winces either absent or minimal.

"No, maybe a week on those."

"Okay. I'm going to send you for some scans and bloodwork. Then I'll be back to see you."

"Thanks, doc."

"Oh, I'm—"

This happens all the time. They see the white coat and think I'm a doctor. It's not worth correcting because they won't.

Those same regrets I have over not reapplying to medical school surface. I was supposed to be an MD. It was the dream. Now it's just a taunt with every instance of someone improperly titling me.

It's common to not get in with your first application cycle. My grades were great as were my test scores, but the feedback was I wasn't well-rounded. I didn't have any extracurricular activities except my fraternity and two years of volunteering at the medical center. No other clubs. No sports. Nothing to make me stand out.

According to one interviewer, book collecting didn't count as a hobby or aid in diversifying my application.

I'd been so butt hurt after that I applied to a physician's assistant school and told myself that was good enough. That it was the next best thing and I should be happy with that. In truth, for the most part, I am, but those regrets still linger. They hang over me like a black cloud waiting to ruin my parade.

"Isaac, who is the general on call tonight?"

Dr. Isaac Ryverdeen is my favorite ED doctor to work with. He stays cool under pressure and has a way of keeping the patients calm. He's no-nonsense but has the goofiest personality when off the clock.

"Why, whatcha got?"

"Pretty sure two has a bowel obstruction. Seems like a pretty decent one, too."

"Yeah?" he peeks around my shoulder, shoving his hands in the pockets of his white coat. We all hate wearing them down here in the ED, but the administration insists on it. "It's Williams. I'll make sure he gets a look at the scans."

"Thanks."

He pats me on the shoulder, flashing me a winning grin before disappearing down the hall.

Clicking into the chart of my next patient, I keep it moving.

It's going to be a long night.

Four drunk college kids, a drug overdose, the flu, a broken arm, and two anxiety attacks later, I'm done.

Hiking my bag over my shoulder, my limbs feel heavier than ever as I make my way to the parking lot.

"Hey, Leighton!" Isaac calls. "Good catch with the obstruction. Should've been an MD," he waves as he speed walks in the opposite direction.

I can only stare after him, watching him slip into his basic sedan and drive off. Most days my insides burn hearing people tell me that very same thing, but I can quickly brush off their words. And today, they sting, too. But it's different. It's deeper. Sharper. So much more painful. Hearing that opinion from someone qualified to have it damn near destroys me.

Those regrets come racing back—ones I can't fix at this stage of my life. I'm thirty-seven. Even if I wanted to, it's too late to go to med school. I'd have to do another graduate program to show recent classroom time and then reapply.

But I wouldn't be any different. There's still nothing else in my life except Gavin and the Richards.

Too bad having a maybe boyfriend won't make me look more well-rounded.

With a sigh, I climb into my own car and speed home. I have a trip to pack for.

Chapter 18

GAVIN

I WAS SURPRISED TO show up at Lee's house ten minutes early and she was still running around throwing stuff into the biggest suitcase I've ever seen.

"Sorry. So sorry," she pats her hands in the air. "I got put on the night shift last night and just ran out of time."

Striding up to her, I pull her into my arms. "Hey, calm down. It's fine. Take your time. We can leave whenever you're done."

She exhales a defeated breath, dropping her forehead just below my chest. "Sure you want me to go?"

Gripping her chin lightly, I force her gaze up to mine. "Yes. I know we're still getting to know each other, but there's a lot we can do there together."

"Like what?" Her arms loosely wrap around my middle before squeezing. The slight pressure bringing our bodies flush. Every bit of concentration needed to keep from standing at attention once again being pressed up against her.

"Hiking. Sightseeing. Snowmobiles. Hot tub." My voice drops a fraction, smirking down at her. The feel of her palms rubbing across my back serving as an instant signal for my cock to stir awake.

I feel like a teenage boy. I've never been this... sensitive.

"I like it." She pulls my head down to hers, our lips meeting in a tender kiss.

Then she moans, and I can't control myself. My mouth consumes hers. Our height difference only testing her ability to grip the rear of my neck.

My hands slip under the curve of her ass, hoisting her in the air before her legs wrap around my waist. I can feel the heat of her pussy through those tiny ass shorts she's wearing, and all I want to do is sink into her. To taste her and hear her call my name over and over again.

"Sweetheart, tell me to stop."

"No," she breathes, crashing her mouth back into mine. Those cute noises surfacing the way they always do when our kiss turns down passion lane.

"If you tempt me..."

"Just a few more minutes," she whispers, her nails clawing at my scalp as her lips suck at the side of my throat.

Strutting into the kitchen, I drop her onto the island counter, capturing her mouth again. She immediately opens up for me, fingers curling around the hem of my shirt before lifting it over my head.

Two fingers slip between us, trailing between her breasts and down her stomach until they find her core. The fabric of her shorts so drenched my fingers come away dripping with her arousal. Her body arches into me as I rub down her seam, then up before pressing my thumb into her clit.

"I wasn't going to go there yet, but now that I know how wet you are, I need just a little."

"Gavin, please."

"I'll give you a choice. My fingers or my tongue."

"Holy shit!" she barks. Whether it's from my question or the tight circles I'm rubbing against her swollen bud is unclear. I don't give a fuck. I need to take just a little bit. Just a tiny taste to hold me over.

"Tongue it is."

Lifting her off the kitchen counter, her legs wrap around me again, her eyes stuck on mine.

I can't get her upstairs fast enough. My mind tossing together fantasies of how it will feel to have her explode on my tongue.

I've always been a giver. And until the last few years of Jen and I's relationship, I'd always had a lot of sex. It seems odd that I've gone without for so long.

Laying her down on the bed, her eyes never leave mine. Kneeling between her slightly spread knees, my fingers curl into the waistband of her shorts. The tips running across her heated flesh. "Do you want this?" My voice is deep, husky, begging. Hoping she says yes because I need this. I need her.

Her fingers reach for my face. The curve of her torso lifting just enough to run her palm over my beard, biting that full lower lip.

"Yes."

Slowly tugging her shorts down her thighs feels like agony. If I thought I could tear the cotton piece of fabric in half, I would. But it might be a bit too soon to destroy clothing.

My eyes bug out of my head when her pussy is revealed to me. "Where are your panties, Leighton?" She only shrugs, attempting to press her legs closed as I slip the shorts over her feet. "No, keep these open for me. I like to get a good look at my food before I eat it."

"Of course you do, you health nut," she groans.

"They do say natural is better." Then I clamp my mouth on my girl's pussy and suck.

The taste of her coats my tongue. *Fuck*, she's so goddamn wet.

Her body arches, fingers curling around the rumpled sheets as I run the flat of my tongue between her lips. "You taste so good, Lee."

Her hum is all I get before she barks out every cuss word in the book as my tongue sinks into her entrance. The pulse of her pelvis up into my face only encouraging me to sink deeper inside her.

Her walls clamp around the intrusion. I have no idea how my dick is going to fit in here when my tongue barely does, but I've always been up to a challenge.

"Gavin," she groans, her nails scratching at my shoulders, trying to find purchase. "Yes. There. Fuck," she moans. "Don't stop. Never stop," she cries out, pumping into my face.

I peer up just in time to catch her teeth sink into that bottom lip. Fuck, I am going to bite that lip next time I kiss her. It takes everything in me not to every time I watch her clamp those perfectly white teeth down onto her flesh.

Going back to work, my tongue swirls inside her, my thumb once again finding her swollen clit. Every hiss, whimper, and moan only makes me work her harder. Faster. Driving her so close to the precipice only to pull back just so this lasts a few minutes longer.

A process I no longer want to continue.

Enough waiting.

I want to feel her come undone on my tongue. Every bit of her release soaking my beard.

"Feed me, Lee," I breathe against her drenched and swollen flesh, only for her to shove her pelvis back into my face.

Sweet arousal coats my lips, my tongue slipping back inside her just in time for her to come undone.

Her body jerks against the bed, heels digging into my back, her thighs clamped around my head as she cries out.

I let it tear through her, drinking her down until her walls only lightly flutter around me. My work is incomplete until I lick her completely clean, swallowing her down as if she's a cool drink of water I need for survival.

Crawling up the bed, I hover over her. She cracks one eye open, her gaze lazily focusing on me. "Is that all I get for now?" she whispers.

"For now." I kiss her forehead, pulling her up with me. "Lets get you cleaned up, then packing. No more distractions."

"Aye, aye, captain," she clumsily salutes me before leading us into the bathroom.

This weekend is either going to be heaven or hell.

If we're lucky, it might be a bit of both.

The drive to the rental only took us three hours. Lee slept most of the time, apologizing with each instance of her stretching awake.

Her lashes beat against her cheeks as she fought off sleep she obviously needed. I got some semblance of rest last night; she worked. My girl was saving lives, in my opinion—no matter how much she claims she didn't.

She told me how her night running around the emergency room drained her. Every description reminding me of the TV shows so many obsess over. Sounds terrifying, but she clearly loves being a medical professional. So I'd told her to sleep. I could entertain myself for the drive, which really just meant listening to financial podcasts. Everything from trends in the stock market to ones focused on entrepreneurs to just basic financial information.

They're boring as hell for some, but to me numbers make sense. Numbers tell a story if you're willing to pay attention. You can manipulate them all you want, but at the end of the day, when handled properly, the numbers will give you the truth.

Pulling up to the house, several cars are already here. The truck is Tyler's. Another country boy at heart. One who never left those roots behind the way I did. He refuses to drive anything but a Ford pickup. Perfect since he often ends up hauling supplies out to the rural areas for the custom barns and stables he builds.

"Hey," I shake Lee's shoulder. "We're here."

She stretches loudly before yawning so wide her jaw pops. Crouching to look out the window, she stares up at the massive house we rented this time.

The exterior reminds me of an authentic cabin, the inside with that same wood finish topped with modern furnishings. The listing said the place sleeps twenty, but we pick based on bedrooms. We've always needed at least seven separate ones, as none of us were willing to share once we started coupling off.

Ace and Nick have both found serious girlfriends since last year. Tyler has been married for five years, and Kian for fifteen. Reed and Craig will be the only single parties this weekend.

This is nothing new for either of them.

Craig doesn't date, and Reed works so damn much that I'm surprised he makes time to be here for these trips. He was the history geek, choosing to go into civil rights law. We've never understood why he stayed here in Ohio for it, but I'm also not complaining about having one of my best friends a few hours away.

"Wow," Lee breathes. "Could you have found a bigger house?"

"Probably," I snicker, climbing out of the car to go open her door. She takes my hand, stepping out, her arm automatically going around my waist. "Come here." Her face turns up to meet mine, giggling when I kiss her.

"Took you long enough!" Craig shouts from the second-story deck, an open beer in hand. I'm not sure if Tyler brought him or Reed, but if he's already been drinking, this is bound to get interesting quick.

"Best friend?" she questions.

Tossing her a wry grin, she only beams at me. "How could you tell?"

"Reminds me of Allie."

"Let's hope not. She told me she was cutting off my balls if I fucked up."

Lee bursts out laughing, kissing my pec before taking my hand.

"Don't fuck up then."

I'm screwed.

Chapter 19

GAVIN

"ARE YOU GOING TO let me help with those?" Lee cocks a brow as I unload our suitcases and her overstuffed duffle from the trunk.

"Nope!" The P popped in a playful tone, but she only eyes me wearily.

Hands reach for the case, forcing me to swing away from her. "Really, let me help. My suitcase weighs a ton."

Abandoning our luggage on the gravel drive, I march up to her, taking her chin between my fingers. "Sweetheart, you're not lifting a finger. Take it or leave it."

Her brows scrunch low, but she says nothing. Releasing her, I cock my chin so she starts off toward the house. The side door propped open with Craig smiling like a lunatic in the doorway.

"I'm guessing you're Valentine's Day," Craig holds out a hand to her. She takes it, shaking twice before shoving it back into her jacket pocket.

"Interesting nickname for me, but unless there was a whole separate portion of his evening before me, then I am she."

Craig's eyebrows shoot to his hairline as he bends forward, cackling. When he calms, he moves out of our way, allowing us through the doorway before throwing an arm around Lee's shoulders. An arm I will break if he doesn't stop touching her.

"Gav, I like her. Can we keep her?"

I only groan, knowing this is a sign he's going to act a fucking fool all weekend. "You can get your arm off her."

"Stop being a grouch," he snorts.

"You sound like Ember."

Craig immediately drops his arm, spinning to face me. The hand with his beer stops in the middle of my chest. "Is she coming? Your sister knows how to have a good time. You guys are all settling down and becoming boring."

My molars grind. I love my best friend. I would take a bullet for him, but there is no way I would ever allow him near my sister. Not a chance. Not ever.

Ember may not fall hard like I do, but she does love hard. She has the biggest heart and will find a way to latch onto the tiniest morsel of good about anyone so she can love them too. It's why she has more friends than the forest has trees. She welcomes everyone, no matter who you are. No matter what you've done.

"She's not invited," I grit out.

"Bummer," he shrugs. "We gave you one of the rooms with the king, so you're not half sleeping on the floor." His cackling laughter rings out again. A running joke since one of our earlier trips and our college days living in the dorms.

"Sorry, but why is that so funny?" Lee questions, slipping a few steps closer to me, effectively putting distance between her and Craig.

Good. She's mine.

"So the first year we did this guys' trip, the cabin we rented only had twin bunk beds. Our fine specimen here," Craig's shoulder bumps mine, "was practically sleeping on the floor because he didn't fit."

"You're not exactly a small guy yourself," Lee eyes him. The bulb of her nose twitches as if she has an itch. A reaction Craig isn't used to when women are around him.

Most grin and giggle, fawning over him. Ready and eager to drop their panties and fuck him with no strings attached.

"Your boyfriend here still has almost five inches on me. I know how to find the fetal position." Craig winks just as Tyler, Reed, and Nick filter in from what looks like a huge living room.

"You made it!" Nick pulls me into a one-armed man hug, ignoring the fact that I'm still holding two suitcases and a bag.

"Good to see you fools, too," I chuckle. "Let me go put our stuff down, and we can catch up."

It's like they hadn't even noticed Lee standing next to me. Maybe in a sea of guys all over six feet, it was easy to miss her. She can't be over five-four, and that might be generous.

"That's not Jen," Reed points.

Fuck, this might be the worst meeting ever.

"No, I'm not. Leighton," she waves awkwardly.

The guys introduce themselves quickly, the tension palpable. "Excuse us," I attempt to shoulder through them. "Where's our room?"

"Second floor, last door on the right," Nick supplies.

"Leighton, you stay down here with us. If our buddy takes you upstairs, we won't see y'all for hours," Tyler deadpans.

She swallows loudly, her mouth opening and closing, and then her voice comes out croaked. "We aren't…"

The room goes silent, every pair of eyes focused on me. "Dude, you got a girlfriend and haven't…" Craig thrusts his hips in the most lude way.

Please let this end right fucking now.

"Fuck off," I growl, cocking my head at Lee to get her to follow me.

She's silent as we move through the house and up the main staircase. The room we enter is massive. The greens, earthy browns, and creams bring out the elegance of the place. It's definitely the nicest house we've rented. I'm guessing the wives picked it.

"I'm sorry," Lee whispers.

"What for?"

She winces, catching my eyes before averting her gaze. "Outing our sex life."

I can only laugh as I kneel in front of her. "Baby, it's fine. I probably should have warned you about them. They have been like this since we met freshman year."

"They are definitely interesting. I'm guessing Craig is one of the single ones."

"You guessed right. He doesn't do relationships."

"I can't imagine a woman who could deal with that all the time." Her hand absently waves through the air.

Sitting on the bed next to her, I link my fingers through hers. "Are you sure you want to be here?"

"And if I didn't want to be?" Her eyes search mine, but I can't read into her expression.

"I'd take you home." An honest answer, though I would hate to come back without her.

Her head tilts to the side before she leans in and kisses me. The soft press of her lips against mine is meant to be sweet, but it quickly turns into something deeper when she slips her hand from mine, her fingers running through my hair.

When she breaks the kiss, she inhales deeply. "I want to be here. I'm just not... well, I can be super awkward around new people, and I don't want them to think..."

"Stop right there. I don't give a damn what they think about us. But I do think I want to kiss you again."

Lee's stare darkens. Those brown eyes are full of desire as she scoots back on the bed, her body leaning into the pillows before she crooks her finger at me.

Kicking off my shoes, I prowl over her, placing kisses up her body until I reach her mouth. "Don't start things we don't have time to finish."

"Who says we don't have time? We're here until Monday, right?" she smirks.

Searching her eyes, there's nothing but burning desire there. She wants this. So do I.

Crashing my mouth to hers, I devour her. That giggle kicking my dick to attention. In a second, my shirt is torn over my head before her fingers fumble with my belt buckle. The clacking of metal and the soft purr of my zipper nearly has me coming in my briefs.

"I want you naked," I kiss up her neck.

Her breath is warm against my ear. The kind of warmth you want to wrap yourself in and never leave. "I'm not stopping you." The sultry wisp of her voice forces my eyelids shut for just a moment. A moment to keep me from tearing into her like an animal.

I'm ready to rip every article of clothing from her body, but I pause. I'd rushed when I ate her pussy earlier. But she's right; we have time, and I'm going to take it.

Crawling off the bed, I tug off my socks and shuck my jeans down my thighs. Her gaze finds my rock-hard dick. The motherfucker throbs, wanting her. Needing her. My tongue knows what it's like to be inside her, but my cock wants to join the club.

Rubbing myself once she groans, those teeth sinking into her bottom lip before I lean over her, prying it free with my thumb. I kiss her softly, teasing and playing with her before dragging her lip between my teeth, her whimper only causing my dick to swell more. "I like this lip." She whimpers again but says nothing more.

Unzipping her coat, she helps me drag it down her arms before it's tossed on the floor. The zip athletic jacket is next to go, revealing her lace bralette underneath. Fuck, the damn thing is sheer, revealing her dark nipples to me. The peaks hardened, just waiting for me to suck and bite.

I'd been so busy staring at her perfect tits I hadn't noticed her drag her leggings down over her thighs. The matching panties staring back at me. "Are you wet, Lee?"

She only nods, kicking her leggings free before spreading her legs wide. And oh fuck, I'm going to damn sure explode looking at her present herself to me. That thin layer of lace doing nothing to hide her arousal. Glistening wet flesh just waiting for me.

Crawling back up the bed, my cheek runs along the inside of her thigh, peppering kisses when she moves against my touch.

"Gavin, please."

"Please, what?"

Her eyes find mine as I run the flat of my tongue over her inner thigh.

"Taste me."

Who am I to deny her?

Chapter 20

LEIGHTON

GAVIN'S SWEATSHIRT DWARFS ME as we make our way downstairs. It smells just like him. As if the fabric was bathed in his cologne and body wash.

My fingers twitch at my sides, eager to lift the sleeve to my nose and inhale, but it's best that I don't act like a complete weirdo on our first vacation.

So maybe his friends were right, but that tongue can do things I've never experienced before, and I wasn't denying myself that for a second time today. By the time he made me come twice, once with his mouth and a second time with a combination of his fingers and tongue, we were a sweaty mess, and his beard was soaked.

Gavin didn't hesitate to usher me into the shower, the two of us laughing the whole time as we tried not to get my hair wet. We failed, hence the messy curly knot atop my head.

"Why are you walking like that?" he whispers as we angle toward the laughter in the living room. The conglomerate of voices coils my already sore muscles that much tighter. Not only in anticipation of meeting the people who mean so much to Gavin, but also for fear I look like I'm walking with a stick up my butt.

"I think your beard took off a layer of my thigh skin," I hiss.

"Mmm," he hums, running the tip of his nose along my cheek, grabbing my hip to pull me against him. "Good old beard burn."

"Yeah, well, this is new for me."

He tenses behind me but kisses my cheek before leading us into the living room. My brain goes into automatic over-analysis mode, wondering what the reaction had been about. It seems to be my new normal since meeting Gavin Norwood. I never cared much about other men I dated, and that's terrifying.

A chorus of "Hey!" greets us. There are more guys than when we walked in, and four women sprawled out next to some of them, each with a drink in hand. Bright smiles point my way, but my lip only trembles, attempting to form my own.

Fuck, I hate meeting new people.

Gavin's large palm presses against my lower back. A point of contact that somehow calms me a fraction. "Everyone, this is Leighton."

"Since when do you have a girlfriend?" a black guy with a bald head snickers, taking a slug of his beer. A familiarity in his features I can't quite place.

A chiseled, gorgeous face like his isn't one you forget. Not with those high cheekbones, cut jaw, and overly full lips.

"Since now." The weight of Gavin's palm slides across my spine, the sweatshirt doing nothing to protect me from the heat of his touch. The butterflies swarming my belly, recalling what we'd done upstairs as his palm grips my hip, pulling me into his side.

"It's about time you got over Jen," another guy with shaggy brown hair and green eyes chimes in.

Gavin tenses next to me again, his fingers flexing. "If we could not mention her this weekend, that would be great. Lee, that's Kian," he points to the black guy, "and his wife, Tonya." The stunning glamazon of a woman next to him waves before raising her wineglass. "Craig, Reed, and Tyler. And that's Ty's wife, Morgan," he points to a bite-sized redhead next to one of the guys I met when we came in. "Ace and his girlfriend Kalla. Nick and his girlfriend Zoe."

"Actually," the woman with pixie features and thick black hair raises her hand. "Fiance!" The other women all squeal, a million and one questions thrown her way, while all the guys hug the man who was sitting next to her.

It feels like utter chaos. My stomach churning, observing the moment. A moment I don't feel like I should be part of. I don't know these people. They don't know me.

This is all so overwhelming. There are so many people, and it is over-stimulating. I hate that Gavin is the only one I know here.

Maybe it was a bad idea to come on this trip. Screw Allie for damn near shoving me out of the comfort of my home. As if my thoughts summoned her, my phone rings. I must have forgotten to turn off the ringer. I always leave it on when I'm doing housework, paranoid I am going to miss some-one needing me in an emergency. A habit that started after Mom's hit and run.

"Excuse me."

I don't think anyone actually heard me as I slip out of the room and onto the open deck. The cold bites at my skin, but I would rather avoid being gawked at while on the phone. Especially when my pulse is bounding and my stomach is in knots. The sense that I'm only seconds from a breakdown makes me suck in sharp breaths as if they'll calm me. They don't.

Bringing the phone to my ear, it takes everything in me not to whimper. "Hey, you! Glad to hear you're alive," Allie quips.

And just like that, my balance has been restored. A sense of calm finding me just hearing my best friend's voice in my ear.

Yet, I can only roll my eyes. Allie has my location. She would know I made it here. "Yes, barely, but yes."

Her tone immediately shifts. The momma bear she's so good at embodying, elbowing her way to the forefront. "What's wrong? Do I need to hit him with my car?"

"No. Nothing like that. You know how I am around people I don't know. And even though I've been getting to know Gavin, there are ten people in this house I've never met. It's just..."

"Overwhelming. I know. Lee, I'm sure they're good people."

"I never said they weren't. I'm just uncomfortable. Not to mention his friends have brought up some woman named Jen twice. I'm guessing it's his ex, but he internally freaks out every time they say her name. Like gets all tense and quiet."

"Lee." Allie's voice is soft. That same comforting tone she uses when I'm on the verge of another depressive dive into oblivion, pummeled by the memory of my parents.

"Dammit, this is why dating is such a pain in the ass."

Her chuckle has me narrowing my glare into the distance. As far as I can see, there are only snow-capped trees and ground. "Because you like him."

"Yeah, I do."

"Look, you need a vacation. You need some downtime. Try to enjoy yourself this weekend. If it's really too much or you're too uncomfortable, you call us, and we will come get you."

A ragged sigh leaves me, my chin dropping to my chest. They always do this. Mike and Allie to the rescue every time life is a little too much for me to handle on my own. Do I really appear that fragile, or are they just that great of people? Does it matter? "Allie, you guys don't have to do that."

"I know we don't, but we will. We love you and just want you to be happy."

"I'm working on it."

"Working on what?" Gavin's voice booms behind me. The buzz of his lips vibrating against one another to stave off the cold reminding me it's the middle of winter in West Virginia, and we should be inside.

"Allie, I gotta go. I will text you later."

"Love you, Bedbug."

"Love you too, Crazy."

I end the call, tucking the phone into the back pocket of my jeans. My body nearly colliding with Gavin's when I spin around to face him.

"Why are you out here?" he questions.

"Allie called."

His brow sinks low, the rake of his gaze over the property slow as if looking for the answers to how my response explains coming outdoors with no shoes or coat. "The house is huge. You could've gone anywhere inside."

"I didn't want to interrupt the celebration."

He says nothing as he pulls me into his arms, leading us back inside and to the living room. Angling us toward an oversized chair, he slips a tumbler of brown liquid into my hand. I'm so busy staring at the contents of the glass that I nearly dump it on myself when he pulls me down into his lap, nuzzling my hair. "It's bourbon and coke," he whispers, kissing the side of my neck.

I take a sip, noticing all the eyes on us. Every single one in the room.

My cheeks heat, gaze casting down to avoid their stares. "What?" I ask.

The redhead woman only shrugs, her voice just as high-pitched as a Disney Princess's. "It's just been a while since we've seen Gavin so happy."

My heart stutters in my chest. Tension pulls my body straight until he forces me to lean back into him. The warmth that is Gavin once again surrounds me, settling me against his front.

"So, Leighton, you went to Ohio State too?" Kian asks.

"Uh, yeah. A year behind Gavin."

Kian only chuckles, pointing in my direction. "I thought you looked familiar."

My head cocks to the side, eyes narrowing on him. "Wait. You were in the suite across the hall who set up the slip and slide outside Morrill, weren't you?"

Kian erupts with laughter, Craig and one of the other guys clapping hands. "Shit, you were there?"

"Yes! Our entire floor went wild that night. You had hair back then, right?"

The room goes silent.

Then Kian chuckles, pecking his wife on the cheek. "Yup! My girl likes me looking like Mr. Clean, though, so it's gone." A large palm rubs his head as his wife shoves him in the chest.

"Don't listen to him. He started going bald in patches at thirty, and his agent told him to shave it off."

More raucous laughter fills the room while Kian mumbles something under his breath.

"Agent for what?" I ask.

"He's a model," Craig mocks, tossing his empty beer bottle into a trash can next to him before cracking another. "If we're going to ask questions, let's make it interesting."

The room groans. "Why do you insist on drinking games every time we get together? We're not twenty anymore," Gavin grumbles, the vibration of his voice shooting through me. A reminder that not long ago, he'd had his face between my legs, and my thighs are burning as we speak.

"Because with booze, so come secrets. First question, worst fear?"

Well, this could be interesting...

Chapter 21

GAVIN

A long exhale leaves me as I sink into the steaming water of the outdoor hot tub. The steam pelts my cheeks as the heat of the water soothes my aching muscles after my torturous workout this morning.

I'd pushed harder than I normally do, determined to bury my negative, whiny thoughts and to work off some... energy. There were no expectations coming into this weekend that anything sexual would happen with Lee, so I needed to make myself as tired as possible. Fatigue the muscles to the point of being useless before I jumped the woman. A partially effective plan.

Letting my head fall back, I attempt to fight off the memories of my mouth on her today. Lee said she would join me soon. After dinner, her nieces video-called her, and she wanted to talk to them. It's clear those two little girls mean everything to her. They're treated as if they were her own.

So here I am in a hot tub alone. Striking fantasies of Lee from my head before she catches me jerking off out here, my thoughts flit back to Craig's version of Twenty Questions.

A shudder whips through me. It seemed as if my friends were determined to bring up the past. Dead-set on reminiscing over the times with Jen I've been trying to keep in the back of my mind for years.

I lived those years, and part of me will always be fond of our time together, but that doesn't mean I need to recall those moments in a torturous loop. It happens every trip, and it's often easy to ignore it. Enough beer and liquor will eventually drown out the noise.

I can't pretend as if she wasn't always there. She was. There's a history and so many good times and laughs.

Today, though, hit like a freight train. Witnessing Lee curl in on herself with every mention of Jen shattered something in me. My past relationship isn't a secret I am trying to keep, but it has no place in my current one, either.

Though my soul believes we've known Lee forever, the truth is it's been two weeks. Rather than spend our conversations talking about the decade-plus I spent with my ex, I wanted to get to know her. And though I know I want to continue to see where this goes, I'm not so disillusioned as to not think my friends could be the reason this doesn't work.

They mean well, but they've only ever seen me with Jen. Every other woman I've tried to date since then hasn't made it past a few months, and I definitely didn't bring them to any of our gatherings.

The swish of water has me peeling my eyes open, Kian settling in across from me.

Every high hope immediately dies. My boys were not the company I wanted tonight.

Like the rest of us, Kian's a jokester, but he's also been married for fifteen years. He can be as serious as he is goofy, and judging by the look on his face, this is bound to be one of his heart-to-hearts.

"You okay?"

"Fine," I grunt.

"Is she okay?"

A heavy sigh leaves me, my head falling back to the edge of the hot tub. "I don't know. I hope so. I think this has been a lot for her."

"You think?" he snickers.

"You've been dating for what? A week? Two? You walk in here and call her your girlfriend and then stick her with all of us and expect her to relax?"

Pressing the heels of my hands into my eyes, it's a fight to block out my friend. A fight to not beat myself up for bringing her here. "It was Ember's idea."

"Don't blame this on your sister."

"Fine. I won't. I wanted her here, too. It's been a while since I felt like this with someone."

Kian nods, running his hands through the water in silence. The quiet stretching between us longer than I would expect. "I don't doubt you've already fallen for her. I've known you for a long time. You always fall hard, but I can tell she's not the type. Give her a little time to catch up to you."

"I hate when you're all perceptive and shit."

He chuckles, and the two of us settle back into silence. The soft whistle of the wind and rustle of trees ease the tension that coiled my muscles tight. The combination is like a lullaby carrying me to sleep when Kian's voice cuts through the night again.

"She's pregnant," he whispers.

"What! I thought the doctors said..." My words trail off. A few years after Kian and Tonya got married, they found out she likely couldn't have children. They'd gone to specialist after specialist. Each one told her the pregnancy wouldn't go to term if she ever became pregnant. So they buried that dream a long time ago.

"I'm terrified."

"Kian." I wish I had more to say. Some sort of insight or reassurance to give, but I've got nothing. Those years when they were spending more time in a doctor's office than anywhere else had been grueling for them. On us too. We worked hard to be a support system for them, but we had nothing to give.

Jen was probably the best at being reassuring, but even she had nothing to truly contribute. Nothing more than love and friendship. Yet, somehow, it was enough at the time.

"We already decided we're going to keep it. See if it'll make it." He sniffles, looking down. "Don't tell the others. T wants to keep it between us for now."

"Of course. If there's anything I can do, let me know. Anything."

He gives me a sad smile, standing from the warmth of the water. "Don't stay out here too long," he nods before disappearing inside.

I can only sit in silence, listening to the sounds of nature surrounding us. My mind whirring, attempting to work through the advice my friend gave me.

So I stay put, giving Lee space. Maybe I've already come on too strong.

Jen said the same thing once upon a time and look how that turned out.

With a sigh, I let my eyes close and just breathe.

It's hours later before I slip back into our bedroom. My teeth clenched tight as I wince against the creak of the hinges.

Lee never came out to join me. Maybe I shouldn't be surprised after what Kian said to me.

Were there signs that this was all too much before we even got here?

Maybe it was the fooling around that pushed her too far. She didn't tell me no, but that first night I stayed over, she said sex was off the table.

Fuck!

The single word roars through my head as my fingers tear at my short hair.

Stupid. So fucking stupid, Gavin!

"Gavin," a raspy groan finds me in the dark.

"Hey, sorry. I didn't mean to wake you."

The rustling of blankets draws my gaze to where I can just make out Lee sitting up in bed. "And that's why you're shouting profanity?"

Double fuck. Apparently, I didn't even keep my outburst in my head.

"Sorry. I'm going to go shower. Go back to sleep."

I disappear into the adjoining bathroom, turning the shower to scalding before stripping out of my swim trunks. Turning to drop them in the sink, I nearly crash through the glass shower door, finding Lee sitting on the bathroom counter with her legs crossed.

"What's wrong?" she questions.

"I—Nothing."

"Liar," she dismisses my pathetic attempt at pretending I'm not hurt she stood me up. Her fingers curl over the counter's edge. The tilt of her torso toward me eating up the space between us. My gaze hungrily raking over her body.

"I was just giving you some space."

She jerks back, those pouty lips turning down into a frown. "Oh. Okay." Her eyes cast downward before she hops off the counter. "Just so you know, I didn't need space from you." Then she nods and turns toward the door.

Reaching for her, my fingers curl around her wrist. "Why didn't you come outside?"

"Yeah, about that. The girls asked me to watch a movie with them, and I fell asleep. It wasn't intentional or anything."

A rumbling laugh escapes me, pulling her into a hug. "Um, I don't know why that's funny. But uh, you're still wet and butt ass naked."

"You act like you haven't seen it before."

"Oh, I have, but I would rather your friends not hear me screaming your name for a second time today. So you shower, and then I'll cuddle you."

I nod, releasing her. She shuffles out of the bathroom, the sound of the TV finding me just before I climb under the spray.

I don't only wash my body clean, but my mind too.

A reset.

We're okay.

Chapter 22

LEIGHTON

The rustling of clothes pulls me out of sleep. The heat that seems to be Gavin's normal is gone. A violent shiver working its way through me despite the gush of toasty air from the vents above.

"Morning, sweetheart. I didn't mean to wake you."

"What time is it?" I snatch my phone from the dresser. The digital numbers blurring before my vision clears.

"Six."

"Ugh," I groan into the pillow. "Isn't this vacation? Why are you up?"

He chuckles, climbing back into bed behind me. That warmth once again draping me in a cocoon I'd happily live in forever. "I told you I run every morning."

"You're such a health nut. It's gross."

His hips flex into me, the semi-rigid length of him pressing between my cheeks. "You could come with me."

"That's a no. That is not the type of cardio I'm into. Have fun, health nut. I sleep in on my days off, you psycho."

"You're cute," he kisses my cheek, then hops out of bed. "Want me to bring you up some coffee?"

The mattress groans beneath me as I flip to my back. "Are your friends up already, too?"

"Ace and Morgan will be. They run with me on these trips."

"So gross. Go away."

"Bye, baby," he kisses me sweetly before walking out the door. The mint of his toothpaste reminding me I hadn't been able to sneak off and brush my teeth this time.

It's another thirty minutes of me tossing and turning before I give up on sleep. Taking a few minutes to freshen up in the bathroom, I ask myself for the millionth time what I'm doing here.

I really like Gavin, but I've never gone on a trip with an ex before. Day excursions to the beach don't count.

Traveling with a partner seems like a big step—a jump toward commitment I'm not sure I'm ready for or how to navigate. Everything about Gavin is new and uncharted territory for me. The unfamiliar threatening to drown me more often than should be normal.

Dark, heavy bags hang under my eyes, and my hair is beyond frizzy, but there was no way I was packing my silk pillowcases and bonnet on a first trip with my...

Dammit. I can't even say the word in my head. It seems too soon. We seem so rushed. Allie always used to tell me it took me so long to love someone they were long gone before I did.

She's not wrong. Allie and a few of my fraternity sisters are the exceptions to that rule. We bonded instantly, and that relationship has remained strong. It was never the same with any of the men I dated. Hell, I'm not even sure I liked most of them.

With a deep breath, I make my way downstairs, the soft chatter of women filtering into my ears.

"Good morning," Tonya groans, sipping from her mug.

"Morning." I give a short wave and tight-lipped smile before sliding onto the stool next to her. The butterflies of the unfamiliar flutter through my belly. Not the type that Gavin gives me, but the ones that leave me digging the heel of my hand into my opposite palm, searching for the right thing to say.

"Morning," Kalla chirps. Tonya nastily grumbling under her breath in response.

I'm surprised I can remember their names this morning. But maybe it's because I spent dinner playing them over and over in my head and then again during Cards Against Humanity afterward. My determination to fit in with them made my focus hard to break. The repetition of rote facts my saving grace last night as much as when I was back in school.

"You don't look like much of a morning person either," Kalla smiles, sliding me a mug of coffee.

My shoulders sag. The energy needed to sit up straight and pretend I'm awake is too much for me. Not with the bright sunlight beaming through the wall of kitchen windows reflecting off the sparkling clean countertops. "I'm not. Not in the slightest."

"That must be fun being with Gav, then. His morning running routine makes me want to vomit," Kalla chuckles, sipping from her mug.

"Um, we're really new, but I will say seeing him up and dressed at six a.m. made me want to gag."

"Aren't you a doctor, though?" Kalla sips again, her elbows resting on the island counter.

"Um, no. I'm a physician's assistant. Similar, but we still operate under a physician's license." A reminder that technically, I can't even make the medical decisions myself because I wasn't good enough to be the one with those two coveted letters behind my name.

"Hmm," she hums, taking another sip.

"What about you two? I never got to ask what you did last night."

Tonya answers first, her tall frame slipping off the stool to rinse her mug in the sink. "I'm Kian's agent. Figured you caught on to that." I nearly spit my coffee out.

"Uh, nope. Missed that part of the joke."

She smiles wide, leaning against the counter. She has a lithe frame, but curves to her. Her matching sweatsuit set fitted enough that you can just visualize the wave of tone to her limbs. "That's how Kian and I met. He was on a trip to New York City. I was already working as an agent and looking for new talent, and well, you've seen him. He became a commodity, and I was representing him, so we were together nearly every day. A year later, he proposed."

"Wow. That's one of those 'I saw this in a movie' type stories."

Tonya smiles fondly, her hand rubbing her stomach. "Something like that." She doesn't shy away from catching my gaze drift down to her flat belly. I've seen countless women do the same, but it's not my place to ask, so I press my lips together, dragging my eyes away.

"And I'm a dance coach," Kalla smirks.

"Dance?"

"Yeah, for a college dance team in Minnesota, where Ace and I live."

"That's very cool."

"Dance is all I've ever known," Kalla shrugs before rinsing her mug, too. "We're heading into town when Morgan gets back. Do you want to come?"

Allie's voice rings through my head. She'd tell me to go. To have fun and live a little.

But this also feels like when our friendship fell apart all those years ago. Sure, we were younger and much less mature, but that sting still lingers just below the surface. I still feel guilty from time to time for drifting away from the best friend this world has ever gifted me.

"You know what?" I chug the rest of my coffee before filling my mug again. "I'd love to."

"Great."

Then I'm left alone in the kitchen, sipping my coffee in peace. The only bit of normalcy I've felt since we got here.

It's another forty minutes before Gavin gets back, finding me in the upstairs loft curled up with a book. I'd been good and only packed two, so I could make the most of the time here. But like him, I have my morning routine on my days off. Coffee, book, journal. If I'm feeling spicy, I'll go to a kickboxing class at the gym.

"Hey, babe," he kisses my forehead, the sweat from his skin streaking across mine.

"How was your run?"

"Refreshing. I'm going to go shower and then we can go do something."

"Actually, Tonya and Kalla asked me to go into town with them." I hate that my voice sounds tentative like I'm asking permission. As natural as things can be between Gavin and me, neither of us knows how to be with each other just yet.

"That's great. Just wait until I get out of the shower so I can see you off."

"Gavin..."

"Please."

Rolling my eyes, I smile and nod before he takes off jogging down the hall. How he still has the energy to move so quickly after how long they were gone is beyond me. Could never be me.

It isn't long before I slip back into our bedroom, catching Gavin just as he's stepping out of the shower. Fat water droplets cling to his light tawny skin. Every feathered muscle is on display, shifting as if they know I'm staring.

Mesmerized by his long toned legs and the round curve of his ass, I can only stare, lowering myself onto the bed. My book falls from my hands, my teeth sinking into my bottom lip, watching him towel himself dry. This is one show I am enjoying far too much to walk away.

He hasn't noticed me yet, but he will. His focus is seemingly on nothing at all. His mind is lost to clarity or thoughts—it's unclear which.

The moment my bottom lip slips free of my teeth, he turns to me, running the towel over his head, and stops.

That ache pounds between my legs as my eyes rake down his body. Memories of his mouth on me playing on repeat. My center eagerly pulsing, desperate to experience what it'll be like to finally have him inside me.

He's denied taking it further than we have so far. Part of me is grateful, the other part wishes he would say "fuck it" again and just ravage me.

"Stop looking at me like that, Leighton," he warns.

"Why?"

Gavin closes the distance between us in two long strides. Bending at the waist, his fists drive into the mattress on either side of my hips. "Two reasons. First, those four women out there will have my balls if I keep you from spending time with them. Two..." His breath fans out over my cheek, the tip of his tongue skimming over my jaw before he kisses me in the sacred spot just behind my ear where it meets my neck. "The first time I have you, no one will be around to hear you scream. So give me a kiss and go downstairs."

My mouth is bone dry. Like the Sahara Desert has never seen a drop of water dry. My tongue swiping across my lips twice, to no avail.

Those long fingers grip my chin. Soft lips press against mine in a firm kiss before his tongue invades my mouth. The taste of his toothpaste and mouthwash explodes on my tongue. The scent of his body wash infiltrating my nostrils as I breathe him in.

The combination of his taste, scent, and still-damp skin is intoxicating. Addictive. Necessary.

My body falls back onto the mattress, his still hovering just close enough that the swollen head of his erection pokes me in the stomach.

Choosing to be bold despite him telling me not to, my fingers curl around his length. My thumb sliding up this thick shaft only to skirt over the swollen head, dragging that bead of moisture with me. His hiss leaves me smiling against his mouth.

"Sweetheart, please."

His voice sounds so pained, but his hips flex into my hand, his mouth claiming mine with the ferocity of a man who's lost all control. Only when his body presses down into mine, do I release him, my palms gripping his bare back, enjoying the feel of his muscles rolling under my touch.

"Lee! Hey, Lee!" a voice yells from just beyond the door.

I can only crack up laughing as he drops his head to my shoulder.

"I'll be out in a minute," I call back to the closed door. "Looks like you got your wish," I giggle, kissing his cheek before slipping out from beneath him.

The whisper of his words stops me at the door. "That wasn't my wish."

I want to turn back, but instead, I leave. My mind twisting the meaning of those words in too many directions for me to handle.

It's girl time.

Later. I'll think about it later.

Chapter 23

LEIGHTON

I swear this group does not know the meaning of vacation.

We shopped at every boutique in the neighboring town before the guys met us for lunch. Our hands were full of bags they all took from us the moment we tumbled out of the lingerie shop, cackling uncontrollably.

Despite not having much of a social life, I have always loved clothing shopping. My mother loved it, and I blame her for my closet full of clothes I never wear but can't help but purchase.

Gavin had only eyed the bags in my hands but said nothing before carrying them for me. The darkening glaze deepened the icy blue of his irises, a sure sign he was curious about what I had bought.

A secret I was determined to keep at the time.

All that shopping did nothing but burn a hole in our wallets and kick up our appetites. Yet Reed insisted we take a historical bus tour before we went out for dinner. Only for Nick to drag us into some hole-in-the-wall bar and buy us more shots than should be possible to consume.

Two was my max.

I'm exhausted.

My feet hurt worse than they ever do after a work shift. Likely due to the heeled booties I packed in an effort to not look like a homeless slob the whole time we were here.

Every muscle in my arms and shoulders ache with unimaginable soreness from buying more shit I don't need, but I've enjoyed Gavin's friends. Except maybe Craig. He's a bit much. Oddly enough, I feel like he and Allie would get along great. The two would probably plot Gavin and I's entire future together if we let them.

Hard pass.

Once we got back to the house, a few of the guys went down to the basement to play pool while everyone else went to bed. Glancing at my watch, it's after midnight. How had we literally spent the whole day out?

"Tired?"

"Exhausted," I admit as Gavin holds me, rubbing my back just inside our bedroom door.

He grabs my bags from the floor, where he set them down when we walked in, dropping them on the loveseat across the room. "Can I look?"

My head shakes, a wide grin pulling at the corner of my mouth. "Knock yourself out."

My feet barely shuffle across the carpet, the effort needed to balance and tear off each boot nearly sending me face-first to the floor. I'm hardly functioning when he hands me one of his t-shirts before stripping out of his own clothes.

"Do you need help?" he chuckles.

I only nod. People really take a lot out of you. After all these years, I would think I'd become desensitized, but it's the opposite. The need to recharge my battery becomes more necessary each time I interact with groups of people.

He's careful, slipping off my socks, then shimmying my jeans down my legs. Heavy, callused palms skimming over my bare skin as he lifts my shirt over my head. Our gazes meeting just as his fingers graze my cheek before cupping my jaw. "You're beautiful. Do you know that?"

I only shake my head. I'm not one of those women who can't take a compliment or anything, but I'm also not so disillusioned to think I'm a supermodel like Tonya.

"Sweetheart, you are." His lips press to the corner of my mouth. "Think you can stay awake long enough to talk a little?"

I'm suddenly alarmingly alert, my heart hammering in my chest. Taking the shirt from his hands, I pull it over my head before sitting on the bed, crossing my legs in front of me.

There's nothing in Gavin's expression to reveal what this conversation will entail. The boulder sitting at the bottom of my gut painfully heavy as I wait.

He stretches out on his side, his body propped up against the pillows and the headboard. "Come here."

Needing to keep my distance, my legs tuck in tighter, hands folded in my lap. "I'm fine here."

His gaze darkens. I've noticed Gavin likes getting his way. He's also a cuddler at all times of the day, not just in bed at night. I'm denying him two things at once, but I want to hear whatever he has to say without the temptation of wanting to ride him until we both come undone.

"I know it makes you uncomfortable to hear about Jen."

"Do you still love her?" I blurt out. I hadn't meant to let my insecurities show, but it's clear she took up a big part of his life. First loves have a way of sticking with you even when you don't want them to.

"No. I fell out of love with her well before we even broke up."

"Okay." My head bobs mindlessly, my gaze focused on my hands. "Okay."

"There are a lot of memories with her for us. I'm sorry that they keep bringing things up, but..."

I wait for him to finish, but he doesn't have to. If we continue this, I'll be stuck with the memory of her. She will be the woman all of his friends and his family measure me against.

"I get it."

He slides closer to me, his legs straddling either side of my body. "But they don't. Everyone thinks I've been moping around these past five years because I'm heartbroken over her or missing her, but it's not that. I miss having someone to love and take care of. I'm not a man built for solitude."

"Tonya mentioned you were a hopeless romantic."

A pregnant silence seems to suck all the air out of the room. The brush of his hands over my bare knees once again heating my insides. "Yeah, I am. I need to ask you something now."

"Go ahead."

"I called you my girlfriend in front of everyone. I need to know... Do you want to be mine?"

The question should be an innocent one. I'm sure people still have the what-are-we conversation. But it's the way he asked that question. That little extra bass in his voice making my insides stir.

Gavin could have asked me to be his girlfriend or to make us official, but no, he'd chosen his words intentionally. Words meant to convey the question isn't that simple. There's a deeper meaning—an iron-clad tie that comes with saying yes.

My lips part, my breaths escaping in heavy bursts. "What does that mean?"

His torso shifts closer, palm running up between my breasts before snaking around my neck to grip the back of my head. My breath hitches as he tugs me toward him. "It would mean I get to take care of you." His lips brush along my jaw. "It means I get to hold you and make you feel good. It means I'm as much yours as you are mine. I don't care about anyone else or want anyone else. It means I am going to want to be near you all the time. So I'm asking you, do you want to be mine?"

The muscles pull around my rib cage. Each deep breath felt with the press of my breasts against my bra. My skin tingling beneath his touch. My internal temperature rising so high that beads of sweat coat my spine and brow.

We both freeze, our breaths held between us. "Yes. Yes, I want to be yours."

His mouth seals over mine, my body scooped up into his lap, knees falling on either side of his hips. His rigid length trapped between us while I shamelessly grind my core against him.

"You need to tell me if I'm ever moving too fast. It doesn't mean I'll slow down, but I'll respect what you need from me."

"Gavin, shut up. I just need you inside me. Right now."

Our mouths meet again, not in the uncontrolled frenzy we found moments ago, but something softer. The kiss of a lover who just got their one wish.

I don't fall fast, but I could.

With him, I know I could, and that's terrifying.

It's possible I might be already.

A thought that's forgotten as he palms my ass, squeezing the supple flesh while running his teeth down the side of my neck.

"Are you sure you want this?"

"Yes. Please. Yes."

My fingers tangle between us, yanking at the band of his briefs, eager to free him.

"Wait." His hands find my biceps, putting space between us.

"What?" I pant.

"I, uh, don't have a condom. Let me go find one."

"You're kidding, right?"

That thick brow scrunches low, his jaw flexing before he answers. "Uh, no." I only groan, falling back on the bed and draping an arm over my eyes. "What?" he questions.

"I'm about to have what's sure to be the best sex of my life, and you stop to go find a condom. Just my luck." Frustration-laced humor lances through my words, though there is nothing funny about this. I finally crave a man like I crave air, and fucking protection gets in the way.

A response a medical professional like me shouldn't have, but my mind is a mess when it comes to the man beside me. Every inhibition and worry thrown out the window with the simplest of touches from him.

"I feel like that's not supposed to be a bad thing."

"It's not," I force out a breath. "Just dammit. I'm going to kick Allie's ass for insisting I put myself out there."

The mattress shifts before Gavin's weight settles against me. His very naked, solid, throbbing dick nestled against my barely there lace panties. "Lee, I need you to answer me very honestly."

"I've been doing that." My tone is a bit more clipped than Gavin deserves. He's trying to be a stand-up guy, and I'm pouting like a child because I want to get laid.

"Fine. Do you want me to go get a condom?"

Now that he's asking, I pause. I've never had a man raw before. I know the risks, but for some reason, I can't seem to care about them. Not with Gavin.

"No."

His hips flex against me, mine rolling in response. A moan released that's embarrassingly loud.

"Do you still want me to make love to you?"

My hand snakes between us, reaching for him. "Yes."

His fingers hook into the band of my panties, pulling them down my legs before he settles between them again. The slight shift of his body causing his length to become soaked in my arousal.

His skin burns against mine. My body pulsing, waiting to feel him stretch me. "I'll ask one more time. Do you want this, Leighton?" His head braces at my entrance, my legs spreading wider, hands on his back, ready for him to push forward.

"I want you. You said you wanted to make love to me, so do it."

Then his hips shift forward, and I see stars.

Chapter 24

GAVIN

I'VE NEVER TAKEN ECSTASY, but I swear the effects would feel like this.

Lee squeezes me tight. Her grip on my back digging in so harshly there might be bruises there in the morning.

I pulse my hips forward again. Her shout answered with her hand clamped over her mouth, mine pressing over top.

"Shh, baby. I don't want anyone to hear the noises you make but me."

I feel like an ass for going back on my promise to her. Our first time together was supposed to be private. A moment just for us. But then I'd seen the desire in her eyes and heard the passion in her voice when she said she wanted to be mine. There was no stopping me then, not if she didn't tell me to.

She only nods, slipping her hand from beneath mine to hold it in place. Her eyes are wide as I slowly withdraw to push in a little further. That muffled groan vibrating through us as her grip on me tightens. It's been so long that I can't recall the last time I had to work this hard to seat myself inside a woman.

"Are you okay?"

She nods again, pushing against my lower back. Her short nails scraping across my skin as her spine bows off the mattress.

I follow the same pattern over and over. A slow retreat, just to push forward a little more. No matter how much further I seem to sink into her, I never make it all the way into her depths. Her walls are clamping down on me too hard. Her pussy is too tight for me to squeeze into.

"Let me in, sweetheart." The words barely escaping through my gritted teeth, no matter how soft I intend them to come out.

She finally releases my hand, hers slipping to the back of my neck. Mouth open, she breathes heavily, meeting me thrust for thrust. Each one is slow and tantalizing. A paced dance between two bodies learning each other for the first time. "Gavin," she pants. "Gav—" Her groan drags out of her as I shift the angle and sink into her. "I don't think you're going to fit."

"It's okay. Not tonight, baby. But I will." I pepper kisses on her lips, her cheek, and her collarbone through my shirt. "Just relax and let me in. You feel so damn good, sweetheart."

She pulls my head down to her, kissing me hungrily.

Time seems to stop as we move together, our pace quickening the closer we draw to our releases. I want her name on my lips. I want to feel her drain me dry.

Leighton is mine. Really mine, and I want everything.

I used to think Jen was it for me, but now that I've had Lee, I can even more confidently say I was wrong. It doesn't matter if everyone thinks it's too soon. I'm already falling for this girl.

"You're close, aren't you?"

She nods, gripping me tighter with both hands behind my neck. Tugging her hands from my skin, I shove her arms above her head. My fingers glide up her skin before weaving our fingers together.

"I can't..." she whimpers.

"You can't what, baby?"

"I've never come without my clit, too."

A grin spreads on my face. There are plenty of women who need the additional stimulation, but with the way she's responding to me, I'm determined to see if I can get her off without it.

"Look at me, Leighton. Just feel me. Okay, baby?" She nods. Our bodies moving in a thrumming beat.

Her fingers curl around my hand that's holding her in place. Her body shaking so violently she could be convulsing. "That's it, baby. Let go."

Her back bows off the bed, mouth open in a silent scream as her orgasm rocks through her. The pump of my hips doesn't slow. My dick swelling with each new thrust. I'm ready to blow. So close to releasing what she does to me.

"Do you want me to pull out?" the words gritted out as I fight to hold back my own release. A question I should have asked before we traveled down this road. Before my balls drew up as my orgasm builds to its crescendo. The flutter of her walls around me coaxing it forward.

"No. I want to feel you."

I want to ask if she's sure again, but there's no time as my muscles flex, and my cum shoots inside her. Heavy jets fill the woman beneath me, who can only lazily smile up at me.

The moment I'm spent, I collapse on top of her, our breathing ragged. Our skin soaked.

Her fingers find their way into my hair again, that soothing scalp massage she often gives me evening out my breathing. It's the best feeling in the world. Being held. Being wanted. Feeling… loved.

"Are you okay?" I grumble against her chest.

"Are you okay?" she slings back at me.

"Seriously, baby," I pant. "Are you okay? It wasn't…"

Her hand finds my cheek, running over my beard the way she often does. "I'm fine. That was…"

"Intense," I supply.

"Exactly." She bites her lip before slipping away from me. "Let's take a quick shower."

Her hand extends to me, her fingers wiggling in my direction.

The first half of the shower proves pointless. We shouldn't have been ready to go again, but we do. Her back plastered against the tile wall as I drive into her.

That first time, I'd made love to the woman of my dreams. But now I fuck her until she can't remember her name.

Now that I've had her, I won't ever get enough.

For the second time since I met Lee, I miss my morning run. Kian even barged into our room, only to find us sound asleep, but we didn't even stir. His text after served as my wake-up call, not his intrusion.

For once, I consciously ignored my routine and just enjoyed the feel of my woman in my arms. I'd tried to be as honest as I could about what it was like being with someone like me. Yet, I still fear she was caught up in the moment and will realize I passively confessed my obsession. As a man who believes in love at first sight, I'd been so close to telling her that truth last night. That what I feel for her is so damn intense I can't breathe.

Fuck, get it together, Gavin.

Snuggling in closer, Lee lets out a sigh as I let sleep claim me again.

When I wake hours later, she's staring at me. Her expression is as if gazing upon a priceless work of art: awe and something like bewilderment holding her features hostage.

What I would do to wake up to her staring at me like that every morning.

"Your eyes are gorgeous," she whispers.

"You're gorgeous," I press my mouth to hers.

We part so much quicker than I would have liked, but her body still presses in flush against mine. "What do you want to do today?"

"Stay in bed with you all day." Those soft curls tickle the bare skin of my shoulder and chest, her t-shirt rising up, exposing her naked core to my leg. My hand slides up her bare thigh, kneading at her flesh. "But if we stay here, I am going to have to have you again, so I was thinking we go back into town today, just you and me."

"But you came here to be with your friends."

Running the tip of my nose along her cheek, she sighs heavily. "We'll have dinner with them, but I also want to spend time with you." Her face pulls back to search mine with my exposed plan.

An emotion shines behind her eyes. One I can't peg as positive or negative before she speaks again. "You said I'm yours, right?" she whispers, picking at the hair smothering my chest. "You meant that?"

"I did."

Brown eyes meet mine. "Then let's go."

Chapter 25

LEIGHTON

IS IT POSSIBLE FOR a man to be perfect?

Gavin's idea of a day in town consisted of buying me more shit I don't need, including two gigantic bags of books I have no room for. Mostly, we'd just wandered around, visiting coffee shops and bakeries.

The key to convincing him to leave behind his health-nut ways.

I was nervous it would be awkward after we had sex, but it seems like we're even more solid. It makes me forget we only met two weeks ago. Days that now feel like a lifetime.

Dinner had been just as eventful as the night before, with everyone pitching in to make the meal. More drinks and laughter than I would think possible amongst twelve people.

It was a night of us retiring early, especially since Ace and Kian were both driving back to Minnesota and New York, respectively. Nick and his new fiance were set to take a detour to a few tourist spots before heading back to Texas.

Leaving the rental had been full of hugs and promises I would come on their trip in the spring. It was surprising to feel like I maybe bonded with these people a little too. The happiness shining behind Gavin's icy blue eyes as I posed for pictures with the ladies only making me that much happier I came with him for the weekend.

Gavin dropped me at home an hour ago. His exaggerated groan in response to drawing the straw to drive Craig back to Ohio and get him to the airport only brought on everyone's laughter. My guy wanted to come back to my place, but I told him I'd call him. I have a shift again tonight, so I want to take the next few hours and veg out on the couch.

A desire that becomes a distant dream when Allie calls out from the front door.

"Back here," I grumble.

She waltzes in wearing the same sweatshirt I tugged on this morning and black leggings. If we put ourselves out there in the world, people will think we purposely dressed as twins.

"Tell me all about the weekend. You barely called, so I know nothing."

"Seriously?"

"Yes, ma'am. Spill. Every. Last. Detail."

So I do. Every moment from when we arrived through to this morning and even him dropping me here at home.

For once, Allie sat quietly and let me go through the events and my feelings without interrupting. A rare occurrence for her. One that puts me on edge.

Retelling it all sounds crazy. More wild than I am imagining it, I hope. As a medical provider, I look for evidence that two things can exist at once. A symptom of one thing and a sign of another.

Gavin and I are moving at the speed of light, and there are so many moments where it terrifies me, or it seems crazy. Like who goes away with a guy and his friends after only two dates?

Me, apparently.

"You're freaking out, aren't you?" Allie clucks her tongue.

"Sometimes."

"Why?"

"Because I think I feel the same way about him?" My lips pout forward, face scrunching, realizing I voiced my admission as a question versus a statement.

"Then you have nothing to worry about. Enjoy the ride." Allie shakes my leg, grinning wide. "From what you said, it sounds like a good one."

"Please, stop," I groan, burrowing my face into a pillow.

She cackles softly. "Come on. I need to make sure you eat before you go to work."

Slipping into my boots, we trek across the front yard. Meals are usually a circus on steroids at Allie's house, but today it's quiet. Mike must have the girls out. My mood darkening not having them here. Since moving next door, I've seen them every day outside of this weekend.

Allie and I sit on the den couch in our favorite spots, downing pasta and reminiscing about our many school memories.

Some of it piecemealed between us because we were so drunk we couldn't recall. The moment so similar to Gavin and his friends this past weekend.

"Do you want us to get you season tickets with us?" Allie asks, sipping her wine.

"Are they already going on sale?"

"Next week."

For some reason, I pause. Before meeting Gavin, I wouldn't have hesitated, but we'd both talked about how excited we were for the football season. Though he only played on the team for a few years, he never stopped cheering for them. Once a Buckeye, always a Buckeye. We go feral for our sports, especially football.

No one loved sports more than my dad. He lived for the high of his favorite teams scoring or the bouts of joy when rival teams lost. The man followed every stat for almost every sport and team. Because of him, sports became my thing too. So, of course, attending one of the best football colleges in the country couldn't have made him any more proud.

The only thing that could have made that man prouder was if I'd played a sport myself. Organized activities were never something that worked well for me, but the dedication to their craft was something I always admired.

A work ethic I studied and adopted with my academics. To be elite, you had to behave as such. So I put everything I had into being the best student I could, and in the end, it still wasn't enough. Proof that we could be viewed as more than a GPA or a list of courses on a piece of paper.

Ultimately, all it resulted in was me never really living. I did nothing out of the ordinary. No extracurricular activities or wild adventures outside of whatever shenanigans Allie and I engaged in on our summer vacations together.

But that's what I've done since meeting Gavin, right?

I've stepped outside of that box of solitude I'd become so comfortable in. As much as my heart and mind aren't ready to admit it, Gavin may be the best thing that could have happened to me outside of leaving behind New York for good.

"I'll get back to you," I whisper. Allie shrugs, taking my plate. She may not have said anything about my hesitation, but she noticed it. My best friend notices everything.

"Thank you for dinner. I'm going to go try to catch a quick nap before I go in."

"Sounds good." She pulls me in close, squeezing me tight. "Happy looks good on you. I love you, Bedbug."

"Love you too, Crazy."

It's another zoo in the ED. I figured working here at the University hospital would be busy, but damn. It never stops. The patient list on my tablet seemingly lengthening, no matter how many patients I work my way through and either transfer to another department or discharge.

I'm still exhausted from the weekend. My thighs are still a bit sore from Gavin's beard, making the nonstop walking uncomfortable. The tender flesh only becoming more irritated the more I race around and begin to sweat.

More than an hour has passed since I requested critical bloodwork on one of my queued patients. A woman who will lie there getting her morphine push and wide spectrum antibiotics until we can figure out what's going on. She lay there writhing for almost two hours before I was even ushered into the room and approved the pain medication.

Nights like this remind me of everything I worked for. The countless hours of studying and clinical rotations prepared me to do my best for these people who believe they are having the worst days of their lives.

That has to be enough.

Dropping into the chair behind the nurses' station, I grin like a fool when my phone vibrates in my pocket.

Gavin: I miss you already.

I read the message several times, waiting for my mind or body to tell me how to feel. My mind still says the clingy behavior is too crazy this early on, but my heart races, and my skin warms. The muscles between my legs clench as if begging him to sink between them again.

"Happy looks good on you." Allie's words ring through my head.

Me: I think I miss you too.

Me: If you play your cards right, I might bring you lunch tomorrow.

Flirting is not my strong suit, but it's probably still necessary even at this age, right? And truthfully, I do want to see him. Even if it is just for a few minutes. That's all I need to feel his arms around me or the press of his lips against mine.

A life of just a few minutes of him at a time wouldn't sustain me in the long term. Not after spending three days together, but it will do for now.

Gavin: Tell me how to play. That's a game I want to win.

A laugh bursts out of me, the nurse sitting at the computer next to me quirking a brow. "Sorry," I wince. Her frown turning to a scowl as I giggle, typing out my message.

Me: Tell me something good.

Gavin: I found a pair of your panties in my suitcase when I unpacked today.

Gavin: Don't worry, I washed them.

My hand claps over my mouth, my eyes wide as I look around the station. As if they would all know what his message said. They wouldn't, but it doesn't stop my skin from heating.

Me: I'm going to need those back.

Gavin: Lunch tomorrow, and I might return them.

I hesitate about what to say next. My body is over-sensitized, and too many emotions soar through me when it comes to Gavin Norwood. This game we're playing either leaves us filled with pleasure or burned beyond recognition.

> **Me: Then you MIGHT get to eat.**

> **Gavin: Just wait until your next day off. I'm going to feast.**

Every fiber of my being ignites. My body temperature skyrocketing high enough I have to fan myself.

> **Me: I'm at work!!!**

> **Gavin: I know. I'm sorry. Forgive me, baby.**

> **Gavin: Have a good shift.**

> **Gavin: Text me if you get a break and when you get home**

> **Me: Yes Dad**

I can only roll my eyes, chuckling as my tablet pings with a patient's results. The vibration of my phone draws my gaze back to the screen. My teeth tugging at my bottom lip, wondering what dirty remark he'll respond with.

Gavin: I'm not old enough for you to call me Daddy

Me: OMG! Bye!!!!!

Every muscle at the base of my belly and between my legs clenches. *Shit*, only book boyfriends say things like that.

No, Lee. Your boyfriend does too.

Tucking my phone back in my pocket, I turn my focus back to my patient and scroll through the labs.

Fuck!

There goes my night.

Chapter 26

GAVIN

As if the weather has, too, found its happiness, the sun shines brightly. The temperature climbing almost fifteen degrees overnight. It's still cold, but the same bite doesn't pinch at your exposed skin.

Hands in my pockets, I jog across the street to the restaurant where Lee is supposed to join me. My meeting finished a few minutes early, so I figured I would get over here and get us a table. I have two hours before I have to get back, but I want to spend every moment with her.

When I told her I would want to be around her all the time, it wasn't an exaggeration. My flesh yearns for her every second of every day, but Kian's reminder stays plastered at the forefront of my mind, too. I need to give her a little time to catch up.

The switch to her being on the night shift this month puts us on opposite schedules, but I refuse to let that deter me. We'll just have to find ways to make it work because I can't lose her. Not yet.

"Two, please," I tell the hostess, following her into the dining room.

She gestures to the two-seater table right beside the window. The warmth of the natural light heating the dark wood and leather-cushioned seats.

Pulling out my phone, I text Lee.

> **Me: I'm at a table by the windows to the left.**

> **Mine: 10 min**

"Gavin!" My name attached to that voice stalls my movements. Every muscle stretched taut momentarily as if I were a robot glitching. My coat hangs halfway down my arms as I slowly rotate in the direction I'd heard my name called.

"Jennifer?"

She's just as gorgeous as she always was. Her auburn hair shimmering in the sunlight, flashing perfectly straight, large white teeth. The specially tailored outfit is a reminder of the high-profile lawyer she has become.

"Long time," my ex smiles fondly before sliding into the chair across from me.

I clear my throat, shuffling in my seat. This isn't the first time I've seen Jen since our relationship ended. Hell, I'm still reminded of her everyday living in what was our condo. Run-ins like this are inevitable, but the last thing I want is for Lee to walk in here and see me sitting with another woman. Especially not the one who made her so uncomfortable all weekend, and she wasn't even there. "How are you?"

"I'm doing well. And you?" Her smile wavers but doesn't leave her face.

"Really good, actually." My grin stretches so wide that my cheeks ache from thinking about my girlfriend.

Before Lee, life was great outside of my love life. Now, it appears all the puzzle pieces are aligning, and I'm terrified of losing it but ecstatic to call it mine.

"You have that glow." Jen swats me with her leather gloves, which are meant to complete her outfit but aren't necessary for today's warmer temperature.

"What glow?"

"The same one you had when we first got together."

My face drops, my torso rigidly shifting back in my chair. Jen's name is poised on my tongue, ready to serve as the first word of my next sentence, when another female voice calls it first.

"Jen, what are you doing here?" Jen stands to hug Lee. The two beaming at each other as if they're old friends.

"Just finishing up lunch. Ran into Gavin here."

"You—"

Lee's words halt. Her eyes dart between me and then Jen. They don't seem to stop moving before a sad smile pulls at the corners of her mouth. "Excuse me."

I'm on my feet in seconds, stopping Lee from running out of here. My arms wrapping tightly around her middle, holding her in place. Whispering against her ear, I hope she'll hear the plea in my voice. That she'll sit and still have lunch with me. "Please stay."

She wiggles out of my grasp, dropping into the chair I'd been in. Her frown deepens with agonizing sadness, dulling those stunning deep amber eyes.

"Leighton. Gavin. It was good to see you both." Then Jen waves, strutting out of the restaurant like she owns the place.

"That was her?"

My head drops as I slide into the chair. "Yes."

"Dammit, Gavin. She looks like a freaking supermodel." The defeated sigh that leaves Lee is enough to pull my gaze up to her. My muscles fighting me every step of the way as if the shame of being caught with my ex is fighting to keep my head down.

Eyes narrowing, my fingers reach for hers, only for Lee to tuck her hands beneath the table. Well out of my reach. Away from my touch. "I don't give a fuck what she looks like."

"How am I..."

"Don't you dare finish that statement. Jen and I are done. She saw me sitting here waiting for you. We barely exchanged pleasantries. I run into her from time to time. We move in the same circles and live and work in the same city. It's going to happen."

I reach for Lee's hand again as she rests them back on the tabletop. Yet again, she pulls them away.

Fuck! I hate this so much. This wasn't how today was supposed to go.

"Let's just eat," she whispers, grabbing the menu from beside her.

"Can I ask you something?" Lee only sighs, her big brown eyes meeting mine. "How do you know Jen?"

"I met her the same night as you at the meetup. She knows one of my fraternity sisters."

Fuck!

Go figure my new girlfriend would become friends with my ex the same night I meet her. Thinking back now, I'd seen Lee talking to a group of women, one I recognized as Jen's close friend Erin. At the time, I thought nothing of it. There are lots of singles in this city, but I somehow missed Jen being in attendance.

"Are you two ready to order?" a server stops at our table.

"Give us a few, please," I tell her, my elbows on the table, hands cupped in front of my face. The woman immediately disappears, her shuffling steps loud in the barely occupied restaurant. "Look, Lee, I want to have a nice lunch with you. Please forget that she was here."

"Where else am I going to find her sprinkled in your life, Gavin? Hmm?" Full lips press into an unforgiving line. The challenge is there in my girl's eyes. A dare to lie to her just to make her feel better in the moment.

Something I absolutely will not do.

I wish she sounded mad instead of defeated. Jen has no place in my life anymore other than being a memory. I wish Lee could see that.

"My condo."

"Excuse me." Lee's torso cranes forward, her chest crushed against the table edge, giving me a better peek at her cleavage in the scoop neck sweater.

"My condo. It's the same one we shared before we broke up."

Lee only flips open the menu, scanning it, her eyes blinking rapidly as if trying to hold back tears. She slams it down moments later. Those eyes drifting back and forth the way they'd done when she first found us here.

"Okay. You're having a burger today. I will lose it if you order another salad. Second, I'm never staying there."

Shoving out of my chair, I'm in Lee's space in seconds, my mouth on hers. The kiss is brief, but I hope it conveys everything my words might not convince her of. I know this conversation might not be over, but I at least need us to be okay in the moment.

"Whatever you want, sweetheart."

Our server returns moments later. We both order burgers, our shared food choice lightening the mood again.

It's fascinating hearing Lee talk about her job. The description she gave of the surgery she got to scrub in on last night turning my stomach. The pink center of my burger is a terrible visual, as I'm told about shredded tissues and gushing blood. But I guess I better get used to it. I'll never be the man who doesn't listen to everything his woman wants to say to him.

Long after we've eaten, we're still there talking, this time reminiscing about football season. Our jersey collections are nearly identical. Fond memories of tailgates and spirit wear remind me that I need to buy tickets for the opening game for everyone. Instead of doing it on our own, each year, one of us guys buys tickets for the whole group. That way, no one misses it, and we're all sitting together.

This year, I'm looking forward to including Lee in those plans.

"So you want to hear something crazy?"

I lean back, smiling widely at her. "Tell me."

"I decided to go through my old pictures, too. There's one of me and Kian the night of the Morrill Tower Halloween Haunt. And there are others of you crowding in with all the guys dressed as superheroes. You were Superman."

A barking laugh bursts free. "It's crazy that we were always right there and never knew each other. Could you imagine?"

"I'm glad I didn't know you then," she drones. "I would have ignored you for my studies."

"Nothing I'm not used to." The words slip free. Memories of how Jen and I first started drifting apart, surfacing.

"I'm not going to ask what that means," Lee says, standing from her seat. "Come on. You have a meeting to get back for."

We leave the restaurant hand in hand, my gaze raking the street, looking for where she parked. "Where's your car?"

"Nope. I'm walking you back to work. My date idea, so I get to walk you home. Figuratively, of course."

Cupping her cheek, a soft brush of my lips over the apple, Lee melts into my touch. "It doesn't work like that, sweetheart."

She only tugs at our linked hands, dragging me behind her. "Come on. Let me see where your office is."

So, with a smile, I follow her lead. We don't talk for the three blocks back, but she never lets go of my hand, that small smile playing on her lips.

"Okay, I'm home. Does walking me to my door come with a goodbye kiss?" I wink.

"Do I get my panties back?"

I shrug, grinning widely. "Maybe tomorrow when I come over."

She presses up on her toes, kissing me hard. "That's all you get then." She winks, too, walking backward away from me, biting that fucking lip again. The short wave when she reaches the corner almost enough to make me run after her.

Finally, turning away from me, watching for the symbol to cross the intersection, I can only stare.

My meeting starts in two minutes, but I can't move. Can't think. I'm fixated on my future as she wanders down the street.

Only when she turns the corner do I head inside, prepared to be distracted for the rest of the day. Five thirty tomorrow can't come fast enough.

Chapter 27

LEIGHTON

So many of us marvel at how quickly time passes.

It doesn't matter if you notice or not. The days fly by. The seasons change, and those same twenty-four hours pass.

Three months have passed since I met Gavin Norwood, and my life has completely changed.

The lonely spells still hit. I still miss my parents so much that some days I can barely breathe. My nieces and work are still the center of my universe. I've reconnected with so many of my friends and forged bonds with Gavin's and the women I met on Valentine's Day, including Jen.

My life is full of people I love, laughter, and endless memories.

No man has ever treated me the way Gavin does. He loves me loudly, even if he's yet to say the words. But more importantly, he has respected the distance I need to put between us and the life he shared with Jen. His friends have done the same. My mind convinced Gavin warned them to.

Regardless, it has allowed me to creep further outside of my shell. To not live our moments comparing myself to the ghost of his first love.

Not once has he taken me to his condo, not even when I caved for a moment because I wanted to see where he lived. *"You said you didn't want to be surrounded by that part of my life. That place means nothing to me anymore. It's just where I occasionally sleep and keep my stuff,"* he whispered while holding me in bed one night.

Back then, I wasn't so sure I believed those words. I figured they were just to make me feel better, but his actions proved otherwise. Gavin and I shared my bed more and more, even during those torturous times I was stuck on the night shift. Those mornings I'd returned home so exhausted I could barely stand. He'd be there waiting to hug me into his chest, usher me into the shower, and then hold me while I slept and he worked from bed.

It wasn't long before I noticed his things migrating to my house, either. His clothing and shoes were left behind in drawers and the closet. Toiletries in the bathroom, and the nasty healthy shit he likes to eat in the fridge.

I said nothing because I enjoyed having him around too much to ask. I didn't want him to think it bothered me or that I was pushing him out because I only wanted to pull him in closer, though it still terrified me.

Plus, despite my health nut preferring more green stuff than I do, having home-cooked meals has been a game changer. My energy is through the roof. The lethargy that often found me after my greasy takeout is no longer an issue even when we do order out. Overall, I just feel better. Whether it's the food or Gavin, it doesn't really matter. I'm the happiest I've ever been.

The blow dryer burns the bare skin of my shoulders as the long strands of my hair whip through the air.

Laziness has allowed my natural loose curls to shine through as of late, but Gavin has a special date planned tonight. Matter of fact, Allie, Mike and his sister are coming too. It'll be my first time meeting her. A meeting I am very nervous about.

Though we were supposed to meet on so many occasions between all our schedules, it's never worked out. So far, all I have are a handful of phone calls to go off of. Another wild child like Allie and Craig set to make roots in my life. How will I ever handle them all?

Gavin has been clear about how close the two are, and it would kill me if we couldn't get along.

Squeals pierce through the buzz of the dryer before arms wrap around my bare legs. "Auntie Lee, Mommy said we can help you with your makeup tonight."

Turning off the dryer, I sit it on the counter before lifting Tori and placing her beside it.

"She did?" My brows shoot high with a goofy grin on my face. "Guess I could use the help then." My niece only nods, watching me part my thick hair into sections so I can straighten and then curl it. She hums to her own beat, entertaining herself the whole time.

"Alright, kiddo. Why don't we go downstairs and eat some pizza and then makeup." She nods again, racing out of the room, screaming Gavin's name.

The two have become almost inseparable. So much so that Mike has been anticipating that Tori is going to ask to trade Dad's soon. I think it's just that Gavin is willing to do all the boring things Tori likes. Puzzles, building intricate Lego figurines and towns, and castle models. His patience with her is out of this world, and I am running out of places to showcase all of their creations.

Making my way downstairs, I pause at one of the pictures lining the stairs. The day I reorganized the shelves in the family room, and Gavin built Tori a throne out of them. Her endless giggles fill my ears as if I've been transported back to the moment. The two important halves of my life existing as one is more than most could ever ask for.

"Hey, babe," Gavin greets me as I shuffle into the kitchen. The warmth of his palm against my lower back burns. The thin button-up night shirt does very little to block out his touch. His mouth lowers close to my ear, the fan of his breath making me hot in ways we can't do anything about right now. "Your hair looks nice." Those firm lips pressing against my cheek so briefly, there was barely any time to blink.

Wrinkling my nose, I avert my gaze. "It's not done yet."

"Still beautiful." Gavin places another swift kiss on my temple, picking up the two plates and carrying them into the dining room. Allie, Mike and the girls are already at the table digging in when we join them.

Tori lists all the things she's going to do to help me with my makeup while Abby rolls her eyes, chastising her sister that it's not the right way. We all laugh at the two bickering. This is what so many dinners have become. The six of us crowded around the table, laughing at nothing.

"Gavin, are you Auntie Lee's husband now?" Tori asks, taking a massive bite of her pizza, her blue eyes large as she stares at him.

I nearly choke, the sips of water taken doing nothing to keep me from coughing. Fire burns my lungs as I fight to breathe.

"Victoria," Mike scolds.

"What? He sleeps in Auntie Lee's bed, and you and Mommy sleep in the same bed, so that makes him her husband, right?"

Allie tries her best to hide her laughter, getting up from the table and pointing toward the kitchen.

"Not yet," Gavin responds just as I'm about to respond.

My eyes find his, the look behind them something I can't quite decipher. It's not an apology. It's not one of those please-play-along type stares he often gives me when trying to tell the girls some wild story, either.

Maybe it's just the same truth I've always seen there.

Slapping my hands against the tabletop, my pulse bounds. The blood racing so fast in response to what just transpired, I can't think. The need to be alone for a few moments driving me to my feet. "Okay, well, I'm full, so I am going to go finish my hair before we get dressed."

I'm quick to exit the dining room. The fun-loving atmosphere that had been there gone with my mood shift.

It's no secret Gavin and I have strong feelings for each other. We all know he fell so fast that the speed of light couldn't have caught him. No doubt he's in this deeper than I am. Rooted in his determination to make sure we continue to work.

But marriage. *Marriage.* Husband and wife. Until death do us part.

That's... more. Bigger. Scarier. Binding.

Jesus, it's only been three months.

That shouldn't be a thought for at least a year, maybe two. Right?

Disappearing into my bathroom, my lungs burn as I try to suck in necessary breaths. The large palm to the center of my back making me drop my head so I don't have to stare at him in the mirror.

Shame courses through me, knowing he feels so much, and I just don't know how to let those feelings go and blossom into something beautiful. My love for another person grows at a snail's pace, and I feel like I'm failing him or defective for being the way I am or for responding the way I did.

"Are you okay?" Gavin whispers.

I nod, sucking in one more deep breath. "Yeah. I'm okay."

He spins me to face him, his arms caging me in, mouth so close to mine, his breaths warm my lips. "Then why did you run off? Was it because I said I was going to marry you?"

"I mean, that's not what you said," I scoff.

"But you know that's what I meant. I, uh, didn't mean today. Or now. Just that..." His voice trails off as if trying to find the right words. "If you wanted to."

Those icy blue eyes meet mine again, swiveling left and then right, then back to center. "I..."

His forehead drops to mine, eyes fluttering shut so his dark lashes fan across his warm skin. "You said you wanted to be mine. I didn't ask you that question lightly."

"I'm just..."

His lips press to my throat. "Not today, but you will be." Then he's gone, snatching the garment bag with his tux off the bed and wandering into the bedroom down the hall.

It's too soon, Lee. Way too soon! Right?

If only my reflection knew that answer.

Chapter 28

GAVIN

CALL ME CRAZY, BUT I've always wanted to take my woman to a masquerade ball. As much as Jen loved to dress up, she would never do anything like this. It was a gaudy show filled with ostentatious gowns she would never wear again.

But when I told Lee there was a fantasy masquerade ball happening in Columbus, she nearly tackled me to the ground and begged for the details.

"This is a book lover's dream!" she'd screeched.

I'd barely pulled up the page with the information on my phone before she had Allie running through her front door for the details, too. So here we are, walking into this hotel ballroom that has been transformed into the most beautiful garden—a fitting theme as our weather has finally firmly settled into warmer temperatures.

The awkward moment that passed between Lee and me at her house seems forgotten as we enter. She and Allie are arm in arm while Mike and I trail behind, our eyes glued to every intricate piece of decor. Even the scent of fresh rain or a waterfall mixed with soft pollen seems to fill the room.

"This is... a lot," Mike swallows.

"Agreed. I figured it would just be like a school dance or something."

The sheer volume of noise in the room is near deafening, forcing Mike to shout over the crowd. "Bar?"

I nod, the two of us letting our women wander out to the dance floor. They don't even bother to glance back, hips swaying as they sing along to whatever song is playing.

It's a battle wedging through the bodies, my phone vibrating in my hand with a text.

Ember: Just got here... where are you????

Me: Headed toward the bar

Me: Back right corner

A minute later, my phone buzzes again.

Ember: Spotted

Arms wrap around me from behind, Mike's brow dropping as he watches another woman touch me. I assumed Allie and Lee mentioned my sister was coming too, but now I can't be sure as his demeanor seems to darken.

"Okay, enough," I pry Ember off me. "Mike, this is my baby sister, Ember."

As if he flipped a switch, his expression instantly settles, and he extends a hand to her.

"Pleasure to meet you. I'm—"

"I know," Ember giggles. "My brother has told me every detail about Leighton's life. This one here," she playfully pinches my nose, "is in love."

Mike's eyes find mine. The question is there in his expression. Yet, I hope I can hide mine from him. The first time I admit I'm in love with Leighton will not be to anyone but her.

Ignoring the conversation that sparks between Ember and Mike, I let my truth flow through me. One that only invigorates me. A truth that could also scare Lee off.

"What can I getcha?" the bartender asks, wiping down the counter as we step forward.

"Margarita and Bud Light," Mike relays, ushering Ember forward.

"Ohh, Margarita sounds great!"

"And you?" he cocks his head my way.

Leaning in over the bar edge, I still have to shout. "Two old fashions."

The guy moves like a mechanical octopus, pouring drink contents and mixing them with an efficiency that seems unnatural. Our drinks slid our way before I could pull cash from my wallet to tip the guy.

Drinks in hand, we wander through the massive ballroom. The fluff of the gowns making it challenging to maneuver through the crowd as we search for our reserved table. A perk I was more than happy to splurge on, knowing the dance floor is the last place I want to be. Unless it's a slow song and I can just sway, you won't catch me out there.

"Not a dancer?" Mike chuckles, taking a deep slug of his beer.

"Absolutely not!"

He only laughs, shaking his head. "Me neither. Allie gives me such a hard time at weddings because I hate dancing."

"Seems like our ladies have it under control." My gaze shifts back to Lee. Her hips sway, arms in the air as she and Allie belt out every word.

I can find the beat just fine, but I have never been comfortable dancing in a crowd. Maybe it's because Jen always outshined me, looking like she was a professional and I was just her prop.

"Way to leave me behind," Ember shoves at my shoulder.

Looking up at her, humor shines in her eyes. "Try keeping up next time." Laughter following my sarcastic reply.

"Rude!" She points my way before taking the seat between Mike and me. "Anyway, you know the Reds aren't going to take that win." She eyes Mike sipping her overflowing lime green drink.

Baseball has always been my sister's sport of choice, so I let her enjoy the back-and-forth taunts with Mike while I keep watch over the room.

It's not long before Allie and Lee drift back into view, twirling together, my girl's eyes finding mine within moments. That broad smile spreads, her eyes twinkling in the dim lights before she makes her way to me.

"Baby, this is Ember."

My sister is on her feet in seconds, pulling Lee into her chest. "I'm so excited to finally meet you."

Gone is the joyous grin. Lee's eyes are wide as she taps my sister's back twice. "Um, hi." Two steps taken to put a manageable distance between her and my overly loving sister. "I'm Leighton. Or Lee. You can call me Lee if that's what Gavin told you." She takes a deep breath as if trying to settle her nerves.

"What do you want me to call you?" Ember tilts her head to the side in question.

"Lee is fine."

"Then, Lee, my friend," Ember hooks her arm through my girlfriend's, "we have a dance floor to tear up."

My eyes plead with Lee, her smile nervous as she chugs behind my sister. The two joining Allie again.

It's another hour of Mike and I drinking and watching the women sweat out their hair and makeup, but Lee has never looked more beautiful. When they make it back to the table, Lee slips her hand into mine, dragging me to my feet.

Her panting breaths push her cleavage high over the rim of the sweetheart neckline. "Come with me," she whispers, bending close to my ear.

Weaving my fingers through hers, Ember flashes a knowing grin, as if she thinks this is going to be some dirty romp in a hotel room.

"You okay, sweetheart?"

"Just need some air," Lee fans her face. "I haven't danced like that since..." Her mouth clamps shut, brow scrunching as if trying to recall what she was going to say. "Geez. It's been three years since the last wedding I went to."

"You only dance at weddings?" I kiss her temple, chuckling. The tang of her salty skin comes alive on my tongue as I lick my lips. My dick twitching in my pants, a reminder that we haven't been alone for the past two days; Tori was insistent on sleeping over so we could finish something called a diamond painting, which is just a bunch of little plastic beads that stick to a picture.

"I guess so," Lee trails off as we exit the front doors of the hotel entrance. Her long, exhaled breath seems to release something from her. The glittering gold of her gown only making her appear as if she's glowing. Her color, she'd said. The cut of the gown clings to every curve of her frame, one that seems to have filled out some since we met. Not a complaint from me. More supple flesh to hold on to is a dream.

"Did I tell you how beautiful you look tonight?"

"You did," she smiles up at me. "But I think I'm okay hearing it again."

"You're beautiful." I kiss her temple, my fingers lightly tugging at the strings of her mask. Mine discarded the moment I settled in at our table. "You're gorgeous." Another kiss to her cheek as it falls away. "You're stunning." My mouth finding the place where her jaw meets her ear. Her moan making me want to pull her body against mine.

My hand finds her waist, fingers flexing. "You're mine." Her lips meet mine, arms slinging around my neck, moaning into my mouth again.

I crush her body against mine, our kiss turning indecent as her fingers thread in my hair. I don't give a shit. There's nothing I wouldn't do for a taste of this woman. Let whoever walks by see us. Let them witness soulmates embracing one another.

"Baby, I really want to take you home."

Her chest rises and falls, heavy panting breaths hitting the exposed skin of my neck as she keeps hold of me.

"I have a better idea. Riskier but better."

She takes my hand, leading us back into the hotel, the concierge smiling wide at us as Lee takes a right, away from the ballroom. She moves quicker than I would think in the heavy ballgown and those massively high-heeled shoes I'd helped her slip into, only stopping when she comes to the single occupancy bathroom.

"Are you suggesting…" The words die on my tongue. I love sex, but not once have I ever done it in public. Jen was adamant about being behind closed doors, as was I.

"If you don't—"

I crush my mouth to hers, blindly reaching for the handle before backing us into the bathroom. The few seconds I spend locking the door, my mouth torn away from hers, feel like agony. Like giving up the sweetest candy known to man. "I've just never done this before."

"Me either…"

"Turn around," I tell her. "Hands on the wall."

She obediently turns. Eagerness has her arms pumping quickly, working to bundle the dress up around her waist. The excessive fabric too much to hold in her hands all at once. When she reaches the hem, she exposes herself to me. The red lace cheeky underwear pressing against the curve of her ass.

Shifting the skirt of her dress into one hand, she braces her palm against the wall with the other. A tantalizing arch of her back pushing her ass up on display before those lust-filled eyes find me over her shoulder.

The pink of her tongue swipes over her wine-painted bottom lip before it's trapped between her teeth. My chest pumping hard, trying to control myself.

Then she smiles. "Now what?"

Chapter 29

LEIGHTON

SOMETHING DARK AND DANGEROUSLY addictive burns behind Gavin's eyes.

The way he bites his lip then releases it before licking his lips hungrily puts my libido into overdrive. The tiny action a mirror to what I'd done moments ago. Only he has a better view. Those icy blue eyes trailing to my nearly bare ass as I swivel my hips just enough to entice him.

My body aches to have his hands on me. To have him sink inside me and claim me the way he does almost every day.

The lace between my legs is soaked. Embarrassingly so. With another shift of my hips, my underwear slips a little further between my cheeks, exposing more of my skin to him. These used to fit a little looser, but I guess since Gavin feeds me non-stop, I've put on a few pounds.

"Gavin," I whine.

"Shh, just give me a minute..."

"For what?" I groan loudly, shifting again. That ache is building. The intensity increasing the longer he leaves me waiting.

I need his hands on me. His mouth. His dick. I need it all.

"To admire my view."

His palm finds one cheek, sliding up over my skin before his fingers slip into the band of my underwear, pulling them down my legs. A trail of kisses left down my thighs, coupled with the scratch of his beard. My new favorite burn.

That raw feeling will follow tomorrow. One I've grown to crave.

Gavin plays no favorites, alternating between my legs until he reaches my ankles, tugging at each one to lift my foot.

"You're beautiful, Leighton."

"You already said that." My words are nothing more than a breathless rasp on my lips. My mouth suddenly dry, anticipating Gavin sinking into me. Filling me. Despite our time together, his girth stretches me beyond what should be normal. It took over a month before he finally seated himself inside me without tears streaming down my cheeks, waiting for the pain to become pleasure.

Since the cabin, we've had more sex than I have in my entire life. He makes love to me. Cherishes and worships my body as if it's the greatest gift he could have been given.

Then, moments like this happen. This darker side comes to the surface. The man who prefers to ravage me and take me quick, shoving to the forefront. One possessed by his need for me. Hungry for every piece of me he'll take.

The hiss of his zipper leaves me moaning so loudly anyone in the hall heard me. They'd know what we're doing behind that door.

"Live a little, Bedbug," Allie's voice rings through my head.

"Lee, sweetheart, I need you to listen to me." I nod. "Look at me." My eyes peel open to find his ruggedly handsome face hovering inches from mine. Allowing my gaze to drift downward, euphoria washes over me, witnessing the veins in his hand bulge, fisting his thick cock. With a swallow, I meet his stare once more. "You know how I feel about you." He tucks a curl behind my ear. "This isn't going to feel like that."

Not once has he ever said something like this to me when this mood overtakes him. The words give me pause now before he kisses my mouth and lines himself up at my entrance from behind.

His swollen head notches at my core, my hips shifting back in the slightest, ready to feel him there. Ready to have him inside me, filling me in a way that only Gavin ever has.

"Please," I whimper.

Where he normally enters me with a soft thrust, Gavin slams home. My hand curls into a fist before the side slams into the wall. "Fuck!" I roar. My throat is instantly raw from yelling out.

There's no time to catch my breath or steady myself against the wall again before Gavin ruts into me. Punishing. Raw. Unbridled.

And fuck, does it feel amazing.

His desire envelopes me. Our bare skin clapping so loudly I'd miss the chant of his name on my lips if I didn't know I was speaking.

"Sweetheart, you feel so damn good. So, so damn good." He slows for a moment, brushing my hair back off my shoulder before palming my breast through the gown. A thumb dipping over the edge, finding my peaked nipples. The brush of the pad over the hardened nub making me hiss through my teeth. Everything is so damn sensitive. "You're doing so good taking me like this. I promise I'll make love to you when we get home."

I only nod, my mouth falling open as he slams into me hard. Then, again and again, pushing on my lower back. The pressure of him inside me only drives me higher as my orgasm builds in my lower belly. Every muscle tightens. My breathing becomes so erratic I feel like I'm on the verge of hyperventilating.

"Gav, I—"

"Just let go, baby. I'll catch you."

A whimper leaves me, my orgasm tearing through me less than a minute later. My knees buckle, but as he said, he's there to catch me. An arm wrapped around my middle, keeping me standing. "That's my girl."

But he doesn't stop, his hips driving into me four more times before he spills inside me. Hot jets of his release filling my core, destined to drip down my legs in a few brief moments.

His back presses against mine, kisses peppered at the back of my head. "Our little secret," I smile.

When we return, only Allie and Mike remain at the table. Mike nods to Ember, who is slow-dancing with a guy on the dance floor. A man she seems to know, as their bodies press into one another, her head resting on his shoulder.

There's something intimate about the moment, but exhaustion is threatening to pull me under, so I put it out of my mind.

A yawn escapes me and Mike in unison just as I'm about to collapse into my chair. A yelp billowing free when Gavin grips my hand and tugs me toward the dance floor. "What are you—"

That large palm settles against the middle of my back, pulling me into his warmth. The scent of the sex we just had mixing with his masculine cologne. "Just dance with me, sweetheart."

"Okay," I nod, wrapping my arms around his neck, my heels finally making it a little easier to hold him like this.

Gavin's deep voice fills my ears. Every word of the song rumbled against my skin. "And with my every last breath, I'm gonna love you to the moon and back."

My chin rises to meet those beautiful eyes. Eyes I could never forget, even if we never saw each other again.

He'd said nothing but the lyrics to the song, but there was something in his tone that made me look up at him. A hidden message there meant just for me. "Did you just—"

"Shh. I don't need you to say it back yet."

I don't get a chance to respond before he clutches me to his chest again, our bodies swaying to the fading beat.

It's funny to think that his declaration of marriage made me lose myself earlier, but hearing him finally say those words only makes me want to hold him closer.

I can't confidently say I feel them yet. Allie's reminders that I love too slow coming to mind.

I can only hope it doesn't take me too long to love Gavin back. A man like him surely won't stick around if he doesn't receive that affection—I assume.

So, I squeeze him tighter. Holding on for dear life. Hopeful that this small moment will convey how strongly I feel about him, even though I can't say the words back. But for the first time in any relationship, I honestly want to.

I've only said them to one man. My first love and long-term relationship. I hadn't meant them when I first said them six months in, but felt that normal pressure that so many of us experience when those dreaded three words come out of our significant other's mouth. In my mind, it wasn't fair to let him think this was one-sided, though at the time, it was.

I didn't want him to think I didn't care, so I said them. I know now it made me a horrible person. It wasn't until a few years into our relationship that I could genuinely say I did. By then, he had waited as long as he planned to. We only lasted another two months before he told me he was done.

Back then, I waited for the heartbreak to follow. Waited to feel like I needed to chase him or plead my case, to beg for more time, but I didn't. I was elbow-deep in my first PA position, so with my exhausting schedule, I didn't feel like I'd lost anything.

I had my parents, and I still spent a good amount of time with my friends. I shrugged and moved on with my life.

Everyone had been so surprised that I was able to brush what we had aside so easily, but for me, once the special ended, it was easy to let go.

Pulling back to look up at Gavin again, I know I won't feel the same way if we end.

Heartbreak will follow this time.

The crippling sort I still battle with over my parents' deaths.

Gavin Norwood has ruined me for anyone else, even if I'm not ready to admit that to myself just yet.

Chapter 30

LEIGHTON

Working the day after partying is the worst. Though we'd been relatively tame, I'm no longer built for it.

We have the boss from hell. Unless you schedule your time off six months in advance, he almost never approves it. If only I'd known there was no chance my request would be approved before I submitted it, I wouldn't have wasted my time.

I'd also tried hard to get my shift covered, but no one who was off wanted to work on a Sunday.

Who could blame them?

I like my downtime just like the next person, but I guess I've also never strictly had Saturdays and Sundays to myself, so it makes no difference to me.

For once, it's a slow day. Thanks to the downpour outside, most of our patients have been slipping and falling. Down steps, on sidewalks, inside stores. You name it, they've come in with their stories.

Works for me. Contusions are easy to treat: Apply an ice pack and go, as long as the patient isn't on blood thinners.

The vibration of my phone buzzes in my pocket, causing a rattling sound against my pen. The incessant *buzz, buzz, buzz* making me grind my molars.

"We'll be in with your prescription shortly, Mrs. Liven." The elderly woman smiles at me, though I know she came in here howling in pain. Passing kidney stones is no joke sometimes. Especially the size of hers.

"Thank you for being so kind to my wife," her husband says, stopping me and cupping his hands around mine. "We are so lucky to have such a nice doctor like you."

I open my mouth to correct him but only smile, patting his hand with my free one. "I'm glad I could help."

That fucking buzzing comes to life again. My smile is tight, dropping my hands into my pockets. "If you'll excuse me."

Disappearing around the corner, I pull my phone from my pocket.

"Hello!" My tone is a little more clipped as I try my best to keep my voice low.

"I'm sorry to keep calling you." Panic coats Gavin's words. His breaths are heavy pants, spiking my heart rate.

Is he hurt? In trouble? *Shit. Not now.*

"What's wrong?" My pulse bounds at my throat, worry pitching my voice high.

He sighs heavily. The sounds of shuffled papers and the click of keys in my ear before he speaks again. "I'm sorry. We can talk when you get home."

"Gavin." My tone is an unforgiving warning. I'm not the type that can operate without knowing what's going on. Patience and calm will elude me unless he tells me why he called.

"My parents are here, and they want to meet you... tonight."

A relieved breath flows out of me. *He's fine. He's fine.* "I'm here until seven and..."

"It's fine. I'll tell them you can't. It's okay..."

"No. No, don't do that." His tone was so apologetic that I don't have the heart to tell him no. If mine were still here, I'd want them to meet him, too. It's only fair. "Why are they here, anyhow?"

"Uh, well, it's my birthday tomorrow."

My mood instantly shifts. "I'm so mad at you."

How had he not told me when his birthday was? There's no way I would have forgotten that. I'm the queen of remembering dates even when they don't serve me.

"I know, sweetheart. Thank you. I will make it up to you."

"Gavin Carson Norwood, you better. I need to go."

"I love you," he breathes before I hang up the phone.

I'm just tucking it back into my pocket, taking several steadying breaths, when I nearly run into Isaac.

"You okay?"

"Oh, yeah. Just..."

"Seemed like a tense phone call." My head rears back. Isaac has always been friendly, but why was he listening to my conversation?

"Were you listening to my call?" My voice comes out low and bothered.

"No, I just overheard you. You sounded upset. Is there anything I can help with?"

"No. It's just... family stuff."

He wrinkles his brow, surely remembering I don't have any biological family left that I claim. This isn't his business, though. We don't have a friendship where I'd tell him anything truly personal.

"Well, there's a good surgery that's about to go up. You in?"

This has become our thing, especially for the patients I help diagnose. I've been in more surgeries than I could have imagined, and I would be lying if I said it didn't make me want to try again. There are plenty who attend medical school at a later age. I could, too... maybe.

That urge to finally put that portion of the past behind me rages. A feeling akin to hope building in my chest, tricking me into believing I could pursue what I always wanted.

Looking down at my watch, it's already six. If I scrub into that surgery, there's no way I'm walking out of here at seven, and I don't want to disappoint Gavin, either.

A tight smile pulls at my mouth. "Maybe next time."

"Huh? You're joking, right?" he calls after me.

"I'm sorry. I have somewhere to be after my shift today." Turning my back on Isaac, I'm eager to get away from this awkward interaction.

"Is that really more important than a surgery?"

I hesitate before answering the question. Torn between my feelings for Gavin and how much happiness he has brought me and what I've always wanted. Slowly spinning back to face my colleague, my mouth presses into that unforgiving line. "It is."

He nods, his hands dipping into the pockets of his white coat. "How about coffee tomorrow, then? I can tell you about it."

There's something in Isaac's tone that makes me wonder if this is about more than surgery. We'd formed a "friendship" on the floor, but not once have we ever eaten or grabbed a coffee together without others around.

"I... can't."

Then I bolt down the hall to the nurses' station, ready to document my last chart before getting out of there.

* * *

My palms sweat, running them down my sides for the umpteenth time as Gavin leads me to the front door of the upscale restaurant his mother chose. One I've never been to, but has what appears to be an amazing menu per their website.

He told me his parents lived in the country, and his mother liked to garden, so I'm surprised she picked a place that requires cocktail attire.

The inside is all dark wood and leather, with dimly lit chandeliers hanging every few feet from the ceiling. Each sconce lining the walls reminding me of decor you'd find in Dracula's castle. I'm suddenly grateful I chose a black dress, so I blend in with the ambiance instead of standing out against it.

Anything to distract from the fact that I am about to meet my boyfriend's parents. A part of relationships I'd always done my hardest to skirt my way around. Lucky for me, it was easy most times, as many of them didn't last long enough to warrant meeting the family, nor did I like them enough to put myself through the borderline anxiety attack I'm having now.

"Relax," Gavin breathes against my ear.

The heat of his breath on my bare skin does nothing to calm my insides. Rather, he riles them up. My body attuned to exactly how much he makes it come alive with something as simple as a single word or a glance.

"I'm trying," I grit out, attempting to keep a pleasant smile on my face. I don't exactly know what his parents look like, and I swear we have been walking through this damn restaurant for what seems like an hour.

I can only hope Ember will be here, too. We hit it off right away last night, exchanging numbers and promising to spend some real time together. She, too, reminds me of Allie. The universe's divine way of surrounding me with the type of people I need most in my life. People determined to bring me out of the shadows and back into the light.

A squeal pulls my attention to the right, slender arms looping around my neck, pulling me into a tight hug. "I'm so glad you're here," Ember grins broadly. "Gav wasn't sure you'd come."

"Em, let her breathe," he sighs. Ember only waves him off, dragging me by the hand.

"Mom, Dad, this is Leighton Bergemont, Gav's girlfriend."

A large man stares back at me, his charming smile seemingly given as freely as his daughter's. He stands, his height towering over me the same way Gavin does, those same blue eyes focused on me. "Luke Norwood," he shakes my hand before gesturing to the gorgeous woman beside him. "And my wife Aisha."

"Hello, dear. " She, too, stands, her palms cupping my shoulders before pulling me into a brief hug. An air kiss to both cheeks follows, leaving my body tense. "It's so nice to finally meet you."

They all sit, Gavin guiding me into a chair between him and Ember.

"Nice to meet you both." I'm sure I look as nervous as I feel, my hands knotting in my lap, fingers twisting painfully over one another. My heart races, unsure what to say or how to act around these people. They seem so different from how I would have pictured them based on Gavin's description. These look like two business moguls, not a corn and wheat farmer and his wife. I think they have cows, too.

"We're so glad you could make it. We know you must be so tired after working all day." His mother smiles wide just as three large goblets of wine are set in front of her, Ember, and myself, with two beers placed in front of Gavin and his father.

As one, they all raise their glasses, their stares locked in our direction. Tentatively, I grab mine, too.

"Happy Birthday," they announce in unison.

My whispered "Happy Birthday" comes seconds after theirs, Gavin's award-winning grin flashing my way. The type that lights up a room and my insides. The corners of his eyes crinkling from years of laughter.

Those lips I'm so addicted to move, but no sound comes out as he mouths his words to me. "Thank you. I love you."

Damn, that shouldn't make me melt.

Chapter 31

GAVIN

Lee's nervousness is so palpable it nearly chokes the both of us alive.

No matter how many times I whisper for her to relax, she only seems to coil tighter. I've noticed she comes off as a bit shy and tentative around new people, but she usually warms up quickly enough.

As this dinner stretches on, the opposite seems to be happening, and I don't know what to do to fix it. I'm unsure if she truly is angry with me for begging her to come out last-minute tonight, following a grueling day at work, or if she's just tired, or if it's *me. Us.* How our relationship took off like an Indy 500 race car. I've never slowed down; I only told her it's okay if she wasn't at the same mile marker at the same time.

She hasn't given any signs that she's having second thoughts about us or is overwhelmed by our relationship, but now I wonder if she's been keeping it in and if this was just the tipping point to our falling apart—a reality I refuse to accept.

"I'm stuffed," my dad rubs his stomach, the area a little fluffier than when I last saw him.

"That's because you ate too much, as always." I chuckle, downing the last inch of my water. This bit of normalcy with my family relaxing me enough that I don't continue to obsess over whether I've driven my girl-friend away.

"Dessert!" Ember chirps. Her hands find Lee's arm, my love's body flinching as if she has never had someone touch her. "Birthday tradition states we each must order a dessert, and it can't be the same as anyone else. The birthday boy or girl goes last but can trade with anyone else at the table."

Lee only stares before the back of her hand finds her mouth, and she starts laughing softly, then louder moments later.

"You're kidding?"

Ember only quirks her head, her expression turning serious. "No..."

"I'm sorry," Lee leans forward, trying to control her laughter. "My Dad used to do something similar. He'd wait for us to order our desserts, order something different, and then end up stealing ours when they were better. I almost forgot about that." Lee's voice trails off as she sobers again. A glassy sheen working its way over her irises.

"Your parents sound like my kind of people," Dad snorts. "We'll have to invite them next time."

Lee goes still at my side, all the humor that had been dancing in her eyes gone.

"Dad!" My outburst causing my mom to rear back as if I'd lost my mind. "Why would you say that?"

He shrugs, as if unsure of what's going on while Lee's head drops. That first sniffle shattering my heart.

"Leighton, dear?" My mother's voice is a soft caress. The same tone she'd used after she'd yelled at my dad for letting us get hurt around the farm.

"I told you her parents passed away not too long ago."

Every bit of color drains from my parent's faces. I know I told them, but they're acting as if I didn't.

"Leighton, I'm so sorry—" My dad starts. Lee's eyes rise to meet his, a single tear streaking down her cheek. One she doesn't even bother to hide.

"Please don't apologize. It's okay. I just..." A shuddering, deep breath leaves her as she wipes the new tears from under her eyes. "It just still hits me hard at random times, but you did nothing wrong, Mr. Norwood."

A thick cloud hangs over the table. Each of us focused on our drinks, but I weave my fingers through Lee's, giving her a soft squeeze. Reassurance, she's not alone. She'll never be alone again if I can help it.

"Um, well, what other traditions should I know about?" Lee suddenly croaks. Our gazes all locked on her red eyes.

Ember leans in close again. "Christmas is the best one. Do you celebrate?"

"Of course," Lee gives a watery chuckle.

"Hey, you never know these days." Lee only shrugs with a nod, a softer sniffle breaking free. "So, part one is the ugly sweater party on the farm. And when I say ugly sweaters, I'm not talking store-bought." My sister pulls her phone free from her purse, swiping through endless pictures until she brings one up.

Without even having to look, I know it was three years ago when I won the contest. The wild mirage of bows and bulbs strung together by tinsel and mistletoe took forever. Not to mention, I'd stitched that wretched sweater myself so I could cover the interior with the massive sewn-in bulb lights they lived by back in the day. They were so bright I needed sunglasses in the dark. The colors illuminating the miniature cows with Christmas hats I'd found at the bargain store and also hand-sewn in every open space.

Lee's hand flies over her mouth, attempting to stifle her laughter. Her eyes water anew, but this time with joy and at my expense.

It doesn't matter. I'd do anything to make the woman beside me smile every second of every day for the rest of our lives.

"We hope you'll join us this year," my mother chuckles.

Lee's eyes meet hers, that sad smile pulling at her lips again. "I wouldn't miss it."

We'd barely climbed into bed before Lee passed out.

For hours I curled into her, holding my woman while she slept. Yet, not once did drowsiness ever take over. Not once have I struggled to sleep beside this woman, but tonight, the memories of her demeanor assault me.

I believe the minor mishap with my parents has been resolved. They apologized so many times that I think Lee was about to lose her composure. But I did, too. Perhaps I'd been the problem and not actually mentioned her parents the way I thought I had.

But there's still that tingling doubt at the back of my skull. The one that tells me maybe we're not on the same page. Maybe I am too much, and Lee has been looking for a chance to distance herself from me. A way out without crushing me.

No longer willing to stare at the ceiling, I peel myself out from underneath her. I've become a pro at doing so and not waking her so I can go on my morning runs, which have dwindled to only three times a week since I started staying here so often. It's not that I don't have the space to run here; it's that I don't want to leave the bed with her still in it. I'm so obsessed with that woman that it's unhealthy, but I do not try to hide it.

Stepping out onto the back porch, the heat of summer simmers in the air. Its warmth does nothing to chase away the negative thoughts filling my head. Even pounding the pavement wouldn't. Experience has taught me as much.

The night seems completely silent. Not even a breeze to rustle the trees. The neighborhood sleeps. No cars creeping down the street or people walking their dogs.

"What are you doing out here?" Lee's gravely voice startles me.

"Did I wake you? I'm sorry."

"No. I had to pee. But why are you out here?" The heels of her hands rub at her eyes as a massive yawn escapes her.

Opening my arms to her, she comes to sit in my lap. The added weight shifting the swing, allowing us to sway lightly. "Just a lot on my mind."

Her fingers pick at my hair, pushing the thick strands back and forth. "About me?" Her head drops the way it had at dinner. That defeated curl of her shoulders nearly breaking me. "I'm sorry I broke down at your birthday dinner. I just... fuck, it sucks that it still hits me so hard sometimes. If I embarrassed you, I'm really, really sorry." The words escape in a devastating rush of emotion. Each one only making me want to pull her closer, but unsure if I should.

"Leighton, stop. Never apologize for missing your parents. This is about me... and you."

She takes a deep breath, her eyes focused on her naked thighs. "You want to break up..." she whispers.

"What! No! Not at all. I thought maybe you did."

Her eyes find mine, wide and confused. "Why would you think that?" Shaking fingers graze my naked chest, the tremble so great I can't help but grab hold to still them.

"Tonight... you seemed tense. Like maybe you didn't want to be there."

Her eyes soften in a way I'm not sure I've seen before. There's a truth on the tip of her tongue. One she would prefer had never come up but is about to spill free. Secrets to unlock this woman I am head over heels in love with.

"I don't like meeting parents." My mouth opens to speak, but she shakes her head, my lips immediately clamping shut. "I always avoided it in relationships. It meant that things were progressing, but except for one guy, I never had those feelings for any of the men I dated. But I do for you, and it makes me feel defective that I still didn't want to meet them because I was nervous and felt like they would see that I'm not in love with you too... yet."

I flinch at her words. I knew that was how she felt, but I wasn't ready to hear them out loud. Still, I cup my hand at the nape of her neck, kissing her softly. "There's nothing wrong with you. I will take you however you will have me. And if the day comes when you know I'm not it for you, I will have to accept that, but I hope we grow together."

"I want that too. I just don't know how to get there."

If anything could shatter my heart, inflicting lasting damage, it's those words.

Chapter 32

LEIGHTON

The sun beats down on my bare shoulders, sweat rolling down my temples and throat. I don't mind the heat, but damn, I don't remember May feeling like a sauna when I went to school here or any of the times I've visited.

When I was a student, May into early June was finals time, so I spent most of my days in the library on the medical campus.

In fact, I can't recall if I ever visited in May. We usually take advantage of my nieces being out of school by the end of the month to go to the beach.

Regardless, I'm making peace with the stifling humidity and pushing on.

My breaths shoot past my parted lips in forceful gusts. I need this walk.

Anything to stop my thoughts from spinning a mile a minute.

Anything to forget how it felt to sit out on the porch with Gavin this morning and suffocate in the panic of thinking he was going to end our relationship. A reaction I've never experienced before with anyone else.

This is the most effective way to forget how it felt like the love we made afterward was more of a goodbye than a confirmation that we were okay and would keep moving forward.

I'm not ready to lose him.

"So…" Allie pants next to me. "We can definitely keep speed walking through the neighborhood for as long as you need, but are you going to tell me what has your panties in a twist?"

My gaze narrows in her direction, but I only push harder. My legs turning over at a quickening pace while my thighs and lungs burn. The sharp edge of my nails bite into my palms as my fists curl into tight balls. Every muscle is tired, screaming in protest from how long we've been out here in the blistering hot sun.

But I can't stop moving. If I do, I'll have to face this.

"Leighton, stop." Allie grabs my arm, forcing me to face her.

I hate that tears prick behind my eyes. Those bastards threatening to showcase my vulnerability and how lost I feel. For once, loneliness isn't an issue, but trying to work through these emotions is. Novelty is not something I am proficient at navigating on my own, and it shows. Every damn day I'm reminded I'm not… normal.

There is no playbook for finally finding people for whom you would give up everything for after losing the most important ones in your life. The instruction manual simply doesn't exist.

I'm a medical provider. I need protocols. I operate using facts and exact measurements. If only love worked the same way.

"Come on, Bedbug. Let's go home."

My best friend takes my hand, turning us in the direction we came from. Her tight squeeze more about keeping me from running away than reassurance.

She's right to keep hold of me. If I could run away from this torment, I would.

It takes much longer to reach my house than I would have thought. My mind was so lost and desperate to get away that I didn't realize how far we'd gone.

Cooler air hits me, only for the drone of the air conditioning unit coming to life to snap me out of my trance. Allie led us inside, and I didn't even notice.

"There, that's better," Allie comes back around the corner. "Let's go change, drink some margaritas, and you can tell me what made you take us on that death walk, kay?"

I don't respond, letting her lead us to my bedroom. Allie quickly pulls out shorts and a T-shirt for the both of us before disappearing into the guest room to grab her undergarments.

It was shortly after we built the bed and added the matching dresser that she claimed a drawer for herself. *"Just in case,"* she'd shrugged while filling the others with things for the girls.

It was unnecessary, seeing as they are right next door, but I guess today it came in handy.

Going through the motions, it doesn't take long to shower and change before sprawling on the family room couch. My eyes drift closed listening to the grind of the ice in the blender and Allie singing whatever her favorite song of the day is. Usually one of our many theme songs from the various vacations we've taken over the years. Each one gets their own tune. It's tradition.

"Okay, up," she coaches, sliding the goblet into my hands.

"Did you make enough?" I scrunch my nose at her.

She shrugs, taking the first sip through the pineapple straw. "Depends on what you have to tell me."

The slushy-cold drink slides onto my tongue. The large gulp is harsh against my throat as I take my first swallow. So cold it burns. "Holy Fuck! How much tequila is in here?"

"Practically the bottle."

"Well, I guess it won't be long before the secrets spill free," I fall back into the cushion, my frozen drink barely staying in the glass.

Allie stretches out across the sofa, her ankles crossed atop my thighs. "I'll try to guess first, and if I do, then we can stop this super shit mood you've got going on today and just enjoy day margs and trash TV."

A laugh bubbles past my lips. Only my best friend could reverse my mood with such nonchalance. Where others might not take kindly to her seemingly dismissing my feelings, I know it's her way of trying to keep me from losing myself in them.

"Okay, so I'm going to guess..." she takes a large swallow. "This is just a stab in the dark," she toasts her glass my way. "You are freaking out because you actually like your boo thang, and the talk of marriage and love makes you feel like you're defective—your words—because of all the other losers you've dated—" I throw her a weary look. "Yeah, I said it, losers—weren't it for you?"

Tossing the straw on the table, I chug half the goblet. *Shit*, I should have known she would hit the nail on the head. She always does. "Are you a mind reader, and you've never told me?" I question, the booze already making my head a bit fuzzy.

"No. Despite what you think about my ridiculousness, I just pay attention. You are the best friend I've ever had. The only sister I ever got. I want you to be happy, and who is going to help you get out of your own way if I don't?"

"I love you too, Crazy," I sigh. "So, what do I do?"

"Seriously?" she squawks.

My body quirks back, unsure what that response was. It was an honest question.

"You have a room full of romance books. Confess your love from the rooftops and then fuck him stupid."

Staring down into my almost empty cup, I nod. We sit there in silence for some time. The both of us draining our goblets only for Allie to fill them again.

I want to be honest with Gavin, I just don't know how to navigate this part of a relationship. But like Allie said, I should just put it out there and see what happens.

Me: Hey...

I scrunch my nose at the stupid text message.

Me: Hi. I know you said you weren't coming back over tonight, but I wonder if you could. I really want to talk to you.

His response is immediate. So fast, I wonder if he'd been waiting for me to reach out first.

Gavin: Are you okay?

Me: I'm fine. I just have something I need to say.

Gavin: Ok… I have a late night but I'll bring something for dinner.

Me: Great. Cya in a bit.

Gavin: I love you.

Those three simple words seize my heart in my chest, and for the first time, I can't wait to say them back.

Chapter 33

GAVIN

I'VE BEEN A NERVOUS wreck all day. No one wants to hear their significant other say, "We need to talk." It doesn't matter how many different ways you can rephrase that dreaded sentence, it never ends well.

I knew it was going to be an insane workday. We had a new Fortune 500 client coming in and another to whom I had to give a final analysis presentation. Another client wanted to have dinner, but I got them to agree to a coffee so I could get to Lee's faster. But it's been nonstop.

My heart is racing, my palms sweaty, and I can barely grip the steering wheel as I make my way to her house—a place that has started to feel like home for me, too.

This morning, she seemed to need space, so I told her I wouldn't be back tonight. It was easy enough to blame this client dinner, and all I had to do today, but the moment she asked me to be there, I couldn't say no. Even if we don't last, I will be here for her. That's how much she has changed my life.

Lee has imprinted herself on my heart, and I can't imagine a life without her, no matter what happens between us romantically. Not to mention I am in love with her nieces. By far the coolest kids.

Ten minutes have passed of me sitting in her driveway, the air conditioning blasting while I yank at my tie. That damn bit of fabric choking me as anxiety knots my insides, torturing me.

I shouldn't be terrified to walk in there, but I am.

My every fiber believes that walking through that door will change my life. There will be no turning back or reversing the outcome of the words that exit that woman's mouth.

Words I'm not ready to hear.

Words I wish I could prepare for.

An outcome that could shoot down so many pathways.

Only when I catch Mike waving from across the yard do I finally cut the engine. No doubt he saw me having a damn near panic attack, thinking my girlfriend is minutes from leaving me without so much as a backward glance.

If he knows I'm here, that means Allie will in seconds, too.

Snatching the flowers I picked up from the seat and the takeout bags, I'm practically hyperventilating as I walk to her front door.

I have a key, but I can't bring myself to use it, instead ringing the doorbell.

The door creaks open, my eyes trailing down Lee's body.

Her hair is bone straight again, and a light dusting of makeup only illuminates her skin as if she's glowing internally. The sundress exposes more skin than I am prepared to see. Usually, if we're ordering takeout, I'm lucky if she even bothers to put on pants. But tonight, she's as radiant as ever.

Dammit. Of course, she would look this good to give me bad news.

"Why didn't you let yourself in?" She quirks her head to the side in question, her grin pulling at one sultry corner of her mouth. A mouth I may never get to kiss again if this talk goes poorly.

"Hands were full," I croak, handing her the bouquet and lifting the bags.

She immediately takes a deep inhale, her smile popping wider.

Confusion distorts my features. She seems too happy to see me.

Yet something inside me won't allow me to believe she actually is.

Sweat plasters my shirt to my back, my body temperature higher than it should be. The anticipation nearly knocking me to my knees, ready to beg her not to walk away from what we have.

"Beer or water?" she calls, disappearing into the kitchen.

"Something stronger?" my voice coming out choked. She leans around the doorframe, cocking a brow at me.

"What have you done with my boyfriend?"

"I—He's—" the words lodge in my throat. I'm so confused by this version of her. My expectation of the somber woman I left this morning is nowhere in sight. Our normal awkwardness is even in hiding.

I didn't plan for a happy Leighton.

Not the pep in her step or that glowing smile on her face and the sparkle in her deep brown eyes.

Is she so happy to end this with me that nothing can bring her down?

I enter the kitchen, dropping the bags on the island. "You said you wanted to talk." My hands tremble, making it nearly impossible to hold the containers as I lift them from the bag and practically drop them on the counter.

"I do, but we can eat first. No need to let it get cold."

"Um, yeah. Okay. I hope Italian is okay."

She groans loudly, her smile stretching wider. "That's perfect. I need a heavy meal. Allie and I had a few too many margaritas this morning."

"I'm sorry, what?"

Lee's hands wave wildly in front of her as she pulls dishes and glasses from the cabinets, her back to me, hiding her face. "I was in my feelings, so she thought we needed to drink through them."

"Uhhh…" I have no idea what to say, so I grab our plates from beside her, stack them high, and then carry them to the dining room table.

She's only moments behind me, bourbon in one glass and water in the other. "I'm not drinking for at least a few days. She used an entire bottle of tequila."

"Thanks." I take the glass from her.

I'd put our plates across from each other the way we normally sit when the girls are here, but she moves next to me, settling on the bench before scooping a forkful of pasta into her mouth.

A moan leaves her as she chews, covering her mouth with her hand instead of using her napkin. I can only watch her as she devours half her plate, talking about the upcoming end-of-year recital for her nieces.

That same pride shines through her eyes with every word. Her love is so pure that I wish I could grab hold of it for myself. She told me she doesn't love me—not yet—but she hopes to in time. It's enough, but it doesn't mean I don't want it any less right now. Here. Today. In this moment.

If she can give me just a fragment of what she has for them, I would be a happy man.

"I'm stuffed," Lee leans back, slightly patting her stomach. "Want to cuddle and watch *Lucifer*?"

I tuck my lips into my mouth, unsure how to approach this. I don't know what to do with her cheerful demeanor. It's not that I haven't seen her like this before, but it just doesn't match the woman I left this morning or what I expected when she texted.

"Look, Lee. I don't know what's going on. You said you wanted to talk, and honestly, I've been losing my damn mind since you texted me, so please just put me out of my misery and tell me what's going on."

My eyes plead with hers, her nerves creeping back in as she grabs my hands. We stand in unison before she leads us out to the back porch, right to the swing where she found me this morning.

"Sit." She gestures, and I do. I hesitate to hold my arms out to her before she sits right beside me, our thighs touching, but nothing more.

The stifling heat hasn't subsided, but as the sun sets, the sky is painted in beautiful hues of pink and purple. A gorgeous scene to accompany words that are sure to shatter me all over again.

"This is all Allie's fault," she starts, toying with the hem of her dress. A little more thigh showing the more she rolls it through her fingers. "She convinced me to move back here and go out on the one day no one wants to be reminded they're alone. But if it weren't for her, I wouldn't have met you. I wouldn't have gotten so much time with my nieces, and I wouldn't have started to heal and live."

"Lee—"

"No, please let me get this out before I lose my nerve." Her eyes meet mine. "Because I will, and then we'll be right back in this weird in-between."

I nod, sliding my fingers over hers. She doesn't pull away. A good sign, maybe.

"Gavin, you are the first man to turn my world upside down, and I don't know what to do about that. I didn't know how to handle feeling so much for you so fast because it's never happened to me. So I ignored it. I pretended like it wasn't real because that was easier than facing yet another big unknown."

My back straightens a little. My ears perk high, eager for her next revelation. But she remains quiet, her fingers tangling with mine before we lock eyes once more. "What are you saying?"

"I'm saying I'm in love with you. I'm saying I love you with my whole heart and every fiber of my being. You have changed me in ways I couldn't imagine, and I will never be able to thank you enough for that, but I can give you this." Her palm flattens against her chest, right over where her heart pumps blood through her body. "I can give you all of me."

I don't wait to pull her into my lap, my lips finding hers. A kiss that seems as much a new start as it does that of two soulmates who have known each other forever.

"I love you so much, Leighton Bergemont."

She smiles down at me, her pouty lips deliciously swollen. "Then let me make love to you for the first time."

Epilogue

LEIGHTON

3 MONTHS LATER...

Bodies flood the High Street sidewalks.

It's not the first time I've walked this main drag since graduating, but this year, it seems different. The fans seem more animated, and the colors of the trees and grass are more vibrant. Every chant of O-H that much louder than it's always been.

Each returned I-O, only making me cackle uncontrollably as I shout beside them.

Game day is no joke at a sports school like OSU.

It's been years since I've been to game day, let alone the opening game. "Excited?" Gavin kisses my cheek.

His—*our*—group of friends all came out. Allie and Mike are joining us with the girls, too. This is literally the ultimate reunion. One I am more than thrilled to experience.

"I am. You know how I feel about football," I grin, wrapping an arm around his waist.

His snort makes me laugh, knowing he's referring to the football romance series I've been plowing through with Allie these past few weeks. Sixteen books of smut and sexy-as-hell football players. It's been a dream.

"Maybe we need to get you back on your health nut diet, so we can try some of those moves out."

Gavin only glares down at me. Since he officially moved in, he's practically stopped running, but we at least make it to the gym together three times a week. He's ditched the salads for actual food and even eats pepperoni pizza with me.

He still cooks for us most nights, but he doesn't prepare everything for a rabbit.

When I asked why he'd changed so much, his response literally tore me apart before putting me back together. *"So many of those things were because I needed to cling to a routine. Something that filled the hole I lived with missing before you."*

The tip of his nose runs along the side of my neck. "I don't need to train like I still play to do everything I want to do with you."

My insides tingle. My core hoping that's a promise for later or maybe even before the game starts. We've also become exhibitionists in a sense since I confessed my feelings for him. It's like we're two teenagers who can't wait to get somewhere private and have loud, filthy sex.

We continue to crack jokes as we make our way to the stadium. We'd done the pregame at a restaurant downtown and then walked up so we didn't have to battle too much traffic. I drove through that mess once, shortly after graduating, and never again.

It's a zoo entering the stadium. That same buzz of game day shooting through my veins. "Reminds me of the good old days." Allie throws an arm around my shoulders, dropping her head so it knocks into mine.

I only snort before wrapping my arm around her waist. "It does, but neighbor, now we have so many more to come."

She throws me a goofy wink before Gavin tugs me into his side. "You have the tickets. I'll meet you at the seats."

"Um, okay."

He places a quick kiss on my cheek before jogging off. When I eye *our* friends, they only stare at me, Craig shrugging in the most exaggerated way with a wide grin on his face. Only for the air to whoosh out of him when Ember backhands him in the chest.

They're acting weird, but I am not going to think about it.

I'm ready for some Buckeye football.

I lead the charge, navigating through the throng of bodies to our lower-level seats. The closest ones I've ever sat in, right along the fifty-yard line.

So many memories race back to me, those joyful tears building behind my eyes. It's been twenty years since I first came to this place, and I never imagined that coming back would completely change my life. Who knew Columbus, Ohio would save me?

My parents are gone, but I've gained a much larger family I couldn't be more thankful for. Each of them already cheering and laughing loudly as we funnel into our seats. The guys shoving at each other and the women rolling their eyes. Even Mike falls in line with them. He, too, has become one of the crew, and it wasn't even intentional.

"Oh, nope!" Ember stops me. "You're sitting on the end with Gavin. He hates center seats."

I only quirk a brow. She's not wrong, but I also know he loathes sitting on the end if there are vendors coming through. He can never stretch out his leg. The same one that ended his football career.

Sliding into my seat, Ember drops next to me.

"This is so exciting!" she squeals.

"What—"

The words stall in my throat as pictures fill the massive screen at the far end of the stadium. Memories frozen in time Gavin and I reminisced over from the years our paths crossed, but we didn't know each other. Then, they suddenly skip ahead to the cabin trip and so many other moments we've captured since then of our lives intertwined.

"What is going on?" I breathe, my pulse racing so fast I'm nervous I'm having a heart attack.

Ember only grabs my biceps, smiling even wider. I find the answer to my question when the screen shows Gavin walking down the stairs with a microphone.

"Leighton Bergemont, you are my whole world." Every eye seems to be on me, my gaze drifting back to our friends, each with their phones out, snapping pictures and taking videos. "My sun rises with you and sets with you." His voice draws closer, and I finally have the nerve to look up the steps as he comes into view. A huge grin splits his face, those blue eyes sparkling with unfathomable adoration. "Everyone told me I fell in love too fast, but I don't regret that. I regret nothing when it comes to how I found you."

He stops in front of me, his eyes burning into mine.

"Lee, I love you. There is no person in this world who has stolen my heart and protected it the way you have. No one who has seen me so clearly and helped me see myself." Then he drops to one knee, pulling a box out of his pocket. The red velvet is a perfect match for the scarlet surrounding us in the stadium. "Our hearts might bleed scarlet and gray, but mine only beats for you. Will you marry me?"

A single tear streaks down my cheek. The world around me comes to a halt. My heartbeat slows, and unimaginable calm washes over me as I extend my hand toward the love of my life.

"Yes!"

Gavin has me in his arms in seconds, the entire stadium erupting in a deafening cheer. I'm not sure how long he holds me, whispering sweet nothings in my ear.

All I know is the pure joy shining in his ice-blue eyes is all I want for the rest of my life.

"When did you?" The words stall in my throat as I fight past the emotion swirling inside me.

Firm lips brush mine, his words a whisper against my mouth. "The day you said you wanted to be mine."

Gripping his cheeks, our mouths collide once more, our smiles wide and carefree. "And to think, it all started at Ohio State."

Also by Britton Brinkley

<u>Misfits Trilogy (with L.A. Scott)</u>

Misunderstood

Misfortune

Accepted

<u>Night Life Duology</u>

Night Life

Night Life 2: Will to Fight

<u>The Company Series</u>

The Tournament

The Target (COMING SOON)

<u>Disavowed Birthright Trilogy</u>

Rise of the Grisym

Dimmer of the Light (COMING 2025)

<u>Fall of the Phoenix Trilogy</u>

Feathers of Truth

Feathers of Destruction

Feathers of Change (COMING 2025)

<u>Scarlet Hearts</u>

Scarlet Hearts

Broken Promises (COMING SOON)

<u>Boulder Ranch</u>

Ride Me (COMING 5-9-25)

Buck Me (by Ashley Willow – COMING 5-9-25)

<u>Dagger & Sword</u>

The Shadows That Shackle (COMING 9-25-25)

<u>The Loyals</u>

The Loyals (COMING 2025)

<u>Baudelaire Blood</u>

Venetia (COMING 2025)

About the author

Britton Brinkley was born in New Jersey and now lives in Northern Virginia.

Growing up an avid reader, the sciences and ancient civilizations mesmerized her. She has always loved immersing herself in new worlds. Britton now enjoys creating her own with her writing buddies Jay Gatsby and the little psycho Artemis Prime (the cats).

Britton's tagline romance remixed is the perfect descriptor for her writing. As a reader of many genres, she writes much the same. The storyline with include romance, but may mix in a few other genres. From fantasy to dystopian, to contemporary,genres, to paranormal and thriller, Britton loves it all. The storyline will mix in romance, but it may also include several other genres.

When she isn't writing, she's likely either reading, watching Criminal Minds, or some other true crime show on Investigation Discovery.

Learn More at BrittonBrinkley.com